Hear My Scare

A.S.Chambers

Acknowledgements

Many thanks to the long-suffering artistic genius that is
Liam Shaw for his awesome artwork

A special thank you to my following Book Club members
for their dedicated support:
Oskin, Karen Woodham (Blazing Minds), Ariion Dragoa,
Melissa, Kevin Denwood, Paul and Mark, Gemma Innes

Also, a shout out to the following Kickstarter backers in
helping this book reach publication:
Charlie Cummings, Sophia, Cheryl Mckibbin, Simon
Brindley, Debs SteamGoth, Lee, Axel Kallesøe, Rebecca
Armstrong, Florentina, Carolyn Smith, Sharon Farrimond,
Adgee Harville, Ron Chick.

Contents

Doing The Right Thing

He hadn't seen a sign of habitation for days.

He had been walking for... how long? He shook his head as he tried to remember. There had once been a time when everything had been so clear, so straightforward. He had been able to say that this was this and that was that. Now though...

Everything had changed.

As the muddy, rutted track along which he walked pulled continually at his filthy, battered boots, he recalled the day that they had been victorious. They had driven the enemy back. The soulless golems had been slaughtered, returned to the ground from which they had been drawn. Oh, there had been a cost, a terrible cost, but a cataclysm had been averted.

Then, as they had stood there, panting from the exertion of the hard-fought battle, they had waited.

And waited.

No trumpet had sounded. No clarion call of victory had resonated through the valley. There was, instead, a deathly silence.

Yet, they all *knew* that the triumphal call had been

1

blown. They all *knew* that their Creator had descended upon his Throne and Heaven had converged with the Physical Realm. In their heads were images, *memories*, of jubilation and celebration. The hero of the hour had walked among them, celebrated and restored. He had returned to be with his kind after his long exile. He had slain his adversary upon the hill above the bloody battleground.

The solitary traveller remembered, alongside these impossible thoughts, gazing up to where the vengeful duel had taken place. He had seen a solitary figure clothed in black atop there and he had immediately gone to their side. Yes, the hero had been victorious in slaying his foe, but something was wrong.

Terribly wrong.

The victor had doubled up in his black robes and screamed before transforming into that which he had slain.

"We are one..."

It was then that everyone on the battlefield felt billions of people begin to die.

Towns and cities had been abandoned, their buildings now bloody mortuaries. Those who had survived the instant slaughter had been herded out into the countryside, away from their useless technology. They had been put to work on the land, a pitiful remnant kept alive for a purpose that the traveller could not comprehend.

And across the world, the monsters that he and his companions had thought dead now walked tall and proud serving their dark master, the one who had orchestrated all this.

He remembered demanding of his kin that they should strike the Black Dragon down while the terrible usurper was new to his throne. They knew where he was.

2

Hear My Scare

They should storm his lair and end it. But his kin had said, "No." They were weary of the bloodshed. They had witnessed too many horrors. So they had returned home, leaving him alone on this rock that hurtled through space around a gaseous ball: a former general now sentenced to exile.

The traveller's thoughts drew to a halt, as did his feet. The Archangel Michael, former general of the army of Heaven, now solitary wanderer of the Divergent Lands, had reached a small village.

It had been a long time since Michael had encountered humans. He had circumnavigated previous villages and hamlets but something drew him into this particular one. He had forgotten how *unregimented* they were. As he made his way into the small settlement, he couldn't help but notice the chaotic nature of their actions. They were not coordinated; they were undisciplined. The villagers constantly bumped into each other as they went about their activities, even though there was plenty of room in which they could manoeuvre. The distribution of workloads seemed uneven and inefficient as some encumbered themselves with more than they were physically capable of whereas others just dawdled.

Was this an intentional effect of the Divergence or had God's favoured species always functioned in this manner? Michael recalled when he had been sent to Earth to watch over his old friend. He decided that yes, they had always been this way. They were little pockets of life that looked after themselves rather than a cohesive, well-oiled machine.

It was no wonder that Kanor had swept them aside with one easy, fell stroke.

3

The Archangel shook his head. No, that was a cruel, heartless observation. The angelic army had at first fared no better when they had encountered the constructs at Megiddo. If it hadn't been for Gabriel's sacrifice…

Michael sighed.

It was better to not think of such things right now. There was a time for remorse and a time for action. The wise soul could differentiate between the two.

And now was definitely a time for action.

Two tired, bedraggled men were hauling a lopsided wagon down the main street of the settlement. As they heaved their load along the rutted track, it bounced and jerked in a terribly unsteady manner. Michael watched as it approached a pothole that was deeper than the rest. By the side of the street, a small, half-starved girl was kneeling in the dirt. She was playing with a handmade doll whilst her mother chatted idly to a friend who was leaning out of a window to a small hovel.

The Archangel's eyes watched as the unsecured load teetered on the edge of the uneven wagon. His honed eyesight saw a bulky sack of heavy produce begin its precipitous arc away from other items. His sharp mind calculated that the sack would tumble out of the wagon and the already pitiful remnant of humanity would be diminished by one.

As the sack began its downward tumble towards the oblivious youngster, Michael had a split second to make a choice.

It was no choice at all.

There was a loud crack as a strangely clothed man seemingly appeared out of nowhere and pulled the young girl out of the gutter. The child screamed as a heavy sack careered off a passing wagon and fell onto her stuffed,

4

ragged toy.

The child's mother cried out and bustled up to her daughter's saviour. Words from her rapidly moving mouth thanked him around tears of relief as she gratefully took her little one from his brown hands.

"It was nothing," Michael whispered. He rolled the bulky sack of produce to one side and pulled a squashed doll from the muddy road. He wiped it clean as best as he could before handing it back to its grateful owner. Heading towards his discarded pack, he explained, "I was just in the right place at the right time." He made to leave but a hand was grasping his arm. He turned and frowned. "I must be on my way."

The woman was saying that he shouldn't. She was insisting that he come and break bread with them. It was only right. He had saved her only child and she had to repay him.

"There is no need," the Archangel insisted as he picked up his pack. "Really, I should be on my way. It would be for the best."

Other villagers were on the street now, watching the commotion. The woman pleaded that he must come to her dwelling and eat. If he did not, she would be considered ungrateful by her fellow villagers. They would regard her with disdain.

Michael's dark eyes studied the tired, ragged assortment of humans that peered up at him. He was in the middle of nowhere, completely off the main route that ran through the country. He looked at the young woman who held the small child in her arms. Her green eyes were pleading for him to stay.

What harm could it do to do the right thing?

"Is this right, Papa?"

Michael smiled as the small girl sowed the tiny seed into the dark earth. "Yes, Annabelle. You're doing very well. The carrot will grow good and strong."

"Just like me," the little one beamed.

"Just like you."

"And Maisie?"

Michael smiled as the small child danced her patched and tattered doll down the drill of carrot seeds. "Maisie, too." He leaned over and ruffled the infant's dark hair. "Now, why don't you finish the row?"

Annabelle grinned and carried on with her gardening as the Archangel watched. Yes, she had certainly grown over the last year. If he had not arrived at the settlement when he had twelve months ago, she certainly wouldn't be sowing reclaimed carrot seed to feed her small family next autumn.

"You're very good at gardening, aren't you?" the small girl said as she carefully dropped another fine seed into the lightly tilled earth.

"Not really. I just picked a few things up along the way. Now, an old friend of mine, Gabriel... He could work wonders with plants."

Annabelle paused in her labours and frowned. "What's wrong?"

"Sorry, sweetie?"

"You look sad."

Michael produced a smile. "It's nothing. Just old thoughts."

"Okay." The little girl simply accepted this vague explanation before resuming the sowing of her seeds, idly chatting to her constant companion fashioned from tattered cloth.

6

Hear My Scare

Michael felt the approach of Annabelle's mother before he heard her soft footsteps. Reaching out with his angelic senses he let himself be washed over in sensations of warmth, affection and love.

Human sensations.

A soft hand touched his shoulder. "How's the gardening going?"

"Exceptionally well." He turned and looked up at the green eyes that regarded him. "How was the meeting?" Even before he asked, he knew. There was the tiniest of creases around those beautiful green orbs. They told of worry and concern. They said that things weren't good.

"The sightings have been confirmed."

Michael let his eyes close. "How far?"

"They're about fifty miles away, as long as the scouts counted correctly."

"Did they use the markers as I instructed them?"

"They say so."

"You don't sound convinced."

"Michael, before you came, we were just a ramshackle bunch of scared people." She settled herself down next to him and slipped her arm through his. "We were frightened rabbits hiding down our burrow terrified that someday soon the hunter would see our small hole and come to explore. You taught us to think differently. You've shown us how to do more than just survive. We are *living*. We have more food than we can eat. We are not getting sick. Our children are growing strong.

"But we are not soldiers."

"I'm not asking you to be."

"Not with words, no. But we can't help but see how you *are*. You are different to us."

"Sally, I told you, I'm just a traveller from the south-ern end of the isle…"

The woman placed callused fingers on his lips. "So you say. So you say. But the way you hold yourself. The way your eyes are constantly alert. The way…"

"What?"

"The way you cry in your sleep. You are a soldier. You have battled and I do not feel it went well."

Michael swallowed. "What do the others say?"

The woman's green eyes twinkled and she gave an amused snort. "They would follow you to the end of the Divergent Lands. No fear lies down to trip their feet when they are with you. You see how they hang on to your in-struction? You hear how they speak your name as if it is a blessing? They know that you can lead us, to turn the tide."

The Archangel shook his head. "No, no, no… They must not think that. All I can do is show you how to protect yourselves; how to live a safe life. There can be no battle."

"But surely there must be? For us to be free we must overthrow *him*." Sally looked quickly left and right and her voice lowered as if the very ground itself was listening. "There is something being said. We heard it from those traders who passed through last week. They spoke of a *Man of Virtue*. There is talk that he will rise and slay the Black Dragon."

Her green eyes held him.

Michael's stomach turned. "What?"

"Do I have to spell it out for you?"

"No. And never speak of this again."

"Why not? It could be you. I know it could. We *all* know it could."

"No. It isn't. I am not this virtuous man. I am just a

simple traveller who has settled here with good people."

"And yet you have inspired us to be so much more than we were before."

"But that does not mean I am your saviour." Michael exhaled heavily. "Anyway. Enough of this. About fifty miles you say?"

"If they used the markers correctly."

"The first rule of combat is to always assume the worst." He rose to his feet. After picking up the small pouch of carrot seeds and tucking them in a pocket, he dusted himself down. "We need to ready the village. The constructs could very well be here tomorrow dawn."

The next morning, the village looked as it had twelve months previous.

At least to the casual observer, that was.

Any healthy produce had been stored in carefully hewn cellars under houses that, on the face of it, were ramshackle hovels. The chipped woodwork and damp thatch hid the true, solid nature of the sturdy dwellings just as the carefully splattered filth along the sides of the roads gave the illusion that the occupants were not concerned with the upkeep of their village. Anyone who passed through would assume that the residents were a broken, sad collection of individuals incapable of working together for the common good.

If this passerby studied a bit harder, they would find accumulated detritus piled up behind these hovels. The visitor would think that this was again a confirmation that those who lived here had no concern for their own well-being. They would not realise that the piles of rubbish were carefully stacked and positioned over healthy crops that were designed to sustain those who had grown them.

As the phalanx of clay constructs marched into the small village, a haughty, smooth-skinned Shadow Wraith riding in front of them, everything seemed to appear as it should. There was nothing of note here — nothing to see.

Yet, when they reached the squalid market square, the Wraith drew his horse to a halt and the constructs stamped to attention behind him, their blank, eyeless visages facing front.

"Who is the leader of this village?" the obsidian-robed rider called out. "I would speak with them."

There was a murmur amongst the assembled villagers until, finally, a green-eyed woman stepped forward. "We don't have a leader, sir," she explained.

"Do you have a name, human?"

"It's Sally, sir."

"Then, *Sally*, you will do." The Wraith turned its horse to face the woman. "Explain what is going on here."

"I'm sorry, sir, I do not understand."

The Wraith appeared to sigh and inclined its head to one side. One of the constructs stepped out of rank and its arm shot forwards, snaking out like a whip. The extended limb snaked around the neck of a man standing nearby and dragged him across the muddy floor to the golem's feet. The villager struggled with his hands against the clay noose and his feet scrabbled in the dirt, but it was pointless. The construct's other arm assumed the shape of a lance and plunged into the man's chest.

Had it been twelve months previous, the village would have erupted into turmoil, with its inhabitants dashing for cover, instinctively running away from the sharpened lances of their oppressor's foot soldiers. But now, they had been trained to do otherwise.

10

Hear My Scare

Each and every one of them stood still, squashing into the lowest pit of their terrified gut any notion of fleeing. To do so would have welcomed pursuit and pursuit would have brought a swift, brutal death.

Instead, they stood still, motionless as the Shadow Wraith surveyed them, suspicion in his eyes.

"A few days back, we passed a group of traders. When challenged, they spoke of a small village where they had been plying their wares. A *thriving* small village." The Wraith's horse stamped underneath him as he circled the woman. "So, here we are to investigate such claims. Yet, what do we find? The usual, so it would appear. Pitiful bags of flesh and bone existing in their usual squalid filth, supposedly eking out a meagre existence until their last day snatches them away and they rot in the ground."

The black stallion drew to a halt.

"So it would appear. On the surface, at least."

The woman's heart fluttered.

"Woman, your face is clean, as are those of your fellow sacks of flesh. Your hair is brushed and groomed. I do not see mud encrusted into your apparel." The Wraith's horse scuffed at the smooth ground with its hoof. "Your roads may be muddy but feel solid and well tended. Not once did I have to steer my horse around a pothole or a puddle on my way into your settlement." He snapped the horse's reins, causing it to screech in a high-pitched whinny and across the top of the equine protest he shouted. "Kill them all!"

The unmistakable sound of clay transforming into deadly weapons filled the ears of the villagers as they continued to hold their positions like well-trained soldiers. The order had not yet been given to dart and grab the weapons that were concealed around the square where

11

their general had known the constructs would assemble. They stood firm in the confidence that all was going to plan.

As the constructs stepped forward to carry out their gruesome task, a tall, dark-skinned man emerged from the crowd. "You will not touch the hair on a single head of these people," he spoke in a low, precise baritone. "They are under my protection."

The Shadow Wraith raised a fist and his troops stood still, awaiting further orders. The leader of the constructs allowed himself a satisfied smile as his tongue slid across his lips. "Ah, yes. Here we are," he purred. "Here is the source of defiance in these pitiful wretches. "Come, angel, show your true form."

The man's eyes burned brightly with fire and his basic, homespun garb shimmered as it transformed into pure white robes adorned with golden armour. Stretching his arms out to his sides, a pair of large, feathery wings spread up from his shoulders. Pointing a finger at the Shadow Wraith he declared, "I am the Archangel Michael, general of the Heavenly Host and you have met your match!"

The Wraith sat calmly on his saddle, the reins of his horse held loosely in his hands. "No," he chuckled. "You are a fool." And, as he said that, the ground around Michael erupted, a sheath of clay enveloping him up to and over his mouth. He attempted to break free and summon his angelic powers but the soft material hardened as a domed head loomed up over his shoulder. "Proceed," the Shadow Wraith instructed.

The constructs did what they were made to do.

The villagers tried to resist. They took up their crudely fashioned armaments, but without the leadership of their immobilised general and his angelic powers, they were no match for the mindless, ruthless golems.

And all Michael could do was watch as they were slaughtered in front of him. He raged internally as he stood impotent within the solid clay restraint, straight-jacketed and bound.

The Wraith cantered his horse up next to the Archangel. "Such a proud species. So arrogant. You still think of us as empty shells only capable of one job: butchery. Remember this, if it had not been for Gabriel and his command of the Potency at Megiddo, my cousins would have won. In fact, they *had* won until he played his little trick. Well, we are a different breed now. We have a different ruler to serve and he learnt well from the Red Dragon's mistakes.

"He knows how to delegate. For an army to be ef-ficient, it needs more than just a grand commander lead-ing the charge into battle. It needs that leader to stand back and watch the bigger picture: those troops that can be seen and those which are secreted in hiding already on the battlefield." The Wraith shook its head. "You angels are all the same. So arrogant. You think you can do it all. This is why you initially lost at Megiddo and this is why you have lost here today. You are programmed to believe you are superior. You cannot think like the underdog. You cannot think like a human.

"That is why Kanor rules this land.

"That is why he will eradicate all talk of a *virtuous man*." The Wraith spat the final two words in the face of his prisoner then turned to a construct that silently ap-proached him, blood dripping from its arms. "Is it done?"

The golem inclined its domed head.

The Shadow Wraith turned his horse and the clay

restraints fell away from Michael. The archangel sank to his knees and blood pooled in the corners of his eyes as he surveyed the carpet of corpses that surrounded him. He became aware of the sound of hoofbeats and regimented marching moving away from him. Turning to the leaving phalanx he cried out, "What of me? Why have you left me alive?"

"Have you not realised?" called out the Shadow Wraith, not even bothering to look back. "You are nothing. You are nobody."

The broken angel watched helplessly as they left him kneeling amongst the bloody carnage.

Waste Not, Want Not

Hi, my name is Josh, and I'm a connoisseur of the subtle taste of sweet human flesh.

I guess, like most things in our lives, it must have begun with my parents, even before I was born.

My father was a banking analyst who spent his work time, and also most of his free time, poring over spreadsheets and databases like a crazed financial alchemist. He then reported back to his employer of the week with minutiae of facts and figures regarding the weaker businesses or investments that they were looking at snapping up and devouring, swallowing them down into the pit of their portfolio's never-sated stomach.

My mother was a liberated, free-spirited individual who created art in the style of retarded six-year-olds. She would wander aimlessly through fields for hours upon end until she found a suitable rock or twig that she would then include in her latest creation, placing it lovingly next to last week's addition — a lump of clay, a piece of moss, whatever had drawn her whimsy seven days previous.

They were, each in their own way, living by the principle that everything had a use, no matter how small or insignificant that item was. My father fed weak, malnourished ventures to his ever-consuming overlords; my mother took nature's detritus and compiled it into something that she saw as beautiful.

However, the longer they spent together, the more they realised that their lifestyles were becoming increasingly less compatible. She, as she saw the whole process of mergers and acquisitions to be quite barbaric, never accompanied my father to the swanky meet-and-greets that his employers hosted where they would peer greedily around the dining room at those less successful than themselves. He, as he was normally too busy fattening up the latest quarry for his financial overlords, never accompanied my mother on week-long retreats into the Cornish countryside where their attendees got high on peyote before spending precious time making friends with every single grain of gravel in the conference centre's courtyard.

About a year before I was born, they made the hard, life-changing decision that something had to give.

It was my father's eighty grand per annum wage.

They had never married, as obviously that would have meant them both surrendering to a patriarchal society that prohibited freedom and burdened individuals with heavy chains of societal rules and mores. What's more, during their time living in a small suburban house in Croydon they had not accumulated much in the way of physical belongings. On the day that they handed over the keys to their house, they gave instructions that what small amount of furniture they had should be distributed to the poor of the parish and that my mother's *objets d'art* were to be left in situ as a welcoming present for the new owners.

So it was that they undertook their grand journey of liberation to the north of England with just the clothes that they were wearing and all that they could carry in a pair of backpacks. To begin with, they lived simply on what nature provided whilst dwelling in a small tent in the Trough of Bowland.

It was idyllic. They awoke every morning to the blissful sound of bleating sheep and the loving embrace of Mother Nature. My mother threw herself into a fit of creativity, the like of which she had never before experienced. Every rock and every unusual stem of grass was greeted with cries of joy and was welcomed into the warm bosom of what she felt would be her greatest of creations. My father was just happy that he no longer had to wear a tie every single day.

This blissful euphoria lasted for approximately six days.

It became quickly apparent that my mother's artwork was suffering from the interminable drizzle and random hungry sheep, both of which are endemic to the countryside around northeast Lancashire. Plus, both my parents decided that they could do with a residence that provided running water.

So it was that they subsequently moved and I was birthed in said running water. Apparently, it was a beautiful experience for the other inhabitants of the self-sustaining residence in the quaint little village just outside a small city in the northwest of England. I was there, obviously, but I cannot recall a single image of the event, even with my mother's later attempts to induce within me a state of total life recollection when I was at the more advanced yet still relatively tender age of six and a half. For my grand entrance into my parents' life of communal sustainability

and low-waste existence, it was decreed that a more con-
ventional birthing pool would not be suitable. This was
due, first, to the notion that the purchase of a paddling
pool was deemed quite a wasteful use of non-biodegrad-
able plastics as it would only have been used once, and,
second, the fact that when my mother suggested alternat-
ively that I could be born in the communal cast iron
bathtub numerous eyebrows were raised in tacit opposi-
tion. So it was that she organised my coming into the
world in the local river. There was quite a fast-flowing current that day and my father had to wade quickly after me
as I started to float away to some rather welcoming yet
decidedly dangerous rapids. Mother said it was a good
omen; I would be strong-willed and independent. Father
provided the counter view that I could have taken a serious knock to the head and been permanently damaged.

I have been told that I attended my first rally at the
tender age of three weeks, two days. Swaddled in a pa-
poose to the front of my life-giver, I was blissfully unaware
of the darling red squirrels that she and the other members of the community were demonstrating for in the
woods just down from our settlement. Unfortunately, so
were the aforementioned squirrels as they had long since
packed their bags and moved out, feeling that the surrounding environs were more suited to their grey cousins.
But, as it is with so many well-intentioned actions in life, it
was the thought that counted.

As I grew, I didn't have the same sort of toys as
children in the city down the road. For them, it was the
likes of Lego and Playstations. However, my mother quite
rightly decreed that these were wasteful nonsenses con-
structed from fossil fuels and the blood of slave labour in
the Third World. So it was that the occasional stick was

my plaything and constant nettle rash my companion as I wandered the local woods under the watchful eyes of grey (not red) Sciuridae.

I suppose it must have been seen by others as a lonely childhood. I was the only offspring on the commune, all the other families foregoing the reproduction of more mouths that would ultimately consume our planet, the men instead wandering off for long walks of solitude and contemplation. I once found Uncle Joe contemplating behind a large tree away from the commune. He looked rather sheepish about the matter. For some reason, it had involved him dropping his trousers and cuddling up to a young woman that I had never seen before from the nearby village. She had giggled quite considerably when I had asked what they were doing, but Uncle Joe had gone very red in the face and had explained that she was just his special friend. I had shrugged and gone on my way. There had been a lot of shouting in the commune that evening and I never saw Uncle Joe again.

Certain members of the commune often came and went. Perhaps they didn't feel it was exactly what they wanted. Who knows? There were, however, those who were stalwarts of our little society, like my mum and dad. One such person was Aunt Bella. A rather portly lady, she suffered from asthma and wheezed when she walked. She refused to take any prescribed medication, saying that it had all been tested on poor little animals and was, in reality, poisonous to humans.

I found her in the woods one day, too.

She wasn't contemplating.

She was dead.

It was a long, hot summer and I was in the twelfth year of my idyllic existence. I had been on one of my normal circuitous rambles through bracken and mud, embraced by the ever-friendly companionship of nettles and listening to the beautiful yet unidentifiable songs of the birds high up in the trees when I saw something through the undergrowth. It was rotund and decidedly bulbous. Carefully, I crept up to it, worried it might be some sort of unknown creature. We did not have access to computers or the internet at the commune due to the pervasive nature of the outside world. It was regarded as a well-known fact that to allow the decadent machinations of the corrupt society outside our utopia even a few centimetres of space on a dreaded mobile phone would lead to the cataclysmic breakdown of our perfect universe. As a result, I was not as well versed in fauna identification as one might expect for an individual who lives in companionable existence with Mother Nature. It was only when I was a few metres away that I recognised the face of my late Aunt Bella, a face contorted in agony and coloured blue from oxygen starvation. It appeared that her own personal universe had been inflicted with its own cataclysmic breakdown. I looked around, unsure as to what I should do, and then I approached the body. Its leg was stuck between a rock and a branch and was twisted at a funny angle with a snapped bone protruding from the torn flesh. As an adult, it is now evident that Bella had caught her leg stuck, tripped and suffered a shock-induced asthma attack. As a child, I just saw someone who I vaguely knew lying still and dead. Over and over, my eyes kept being drawn back to the open wound. It was so wet, so red, with the white shard of bone sticking through the lacerated skin. I touched the tip of the bone. It was hard and unforgiving. My fingers came away red. The blood had stained my skin and I unthinkingly shoved my finger in my mouth to clean it.

The taste of the liquid was a revelation.

Never before had something caused such emotion inside of me. My brain exploded and my taste buds tingled at the new experience. I pulled my finger out of my mouth and regarded the broken leg once more. I drew my finger across the wound, gathering up more of the blood, and eagerly wiped it over my tongue. This time, I even expelled a low moan of pleasure!

This stuff was amazing!

And there was so much of it...

I pushed my finger deep into the wound and drew out more congealed blood. But that was not all. This time there was tissue matter on my digit. I dropped it into my mouth and chewed slowly.

It tasted so good.

It seemed a shame to let it all go to waste.

When they eventually found Aunt Bella, it was decided that a wild animal had eaten most of her left leg.

I said nothing.

For the rest of that summer, I found it increasingly harder and harder to sleep. Mother said that it was because, at the tender age of twelve, I was growing into manhood. She explained in graphic detail what I should expect to find staining my bedsheets soon and why it was there. I recall that halfway through the lecture I phased out and just recalled the sweet taste of Aunt Bella between my ripping and grinding teeth. I knew that this was the real reason that my sleep was evading me.

I needed more of that tender feast.

A week or so later, a family of three moved into Bella's dwelling. Their son, Thomas, was a year younger than me and never shut up. He would follow me around the commune constantly ratting off banal questions to which I had neither interest nor answer. For so long, I had been used to being the only child and the peacefulness had been blissful. Now this solitude had been shattered, and I didn't like it, not one little bit.

One day, Thomas followed me out into the woods. He was whiffling on about something and some such. My ears heard the sounds but my brain did not listen to the words. Instead, there were just colours flowing around inside my mind: reds and scarlets, pinks and crimsons. They smelt divine and my stomach was rumbling. We had been walking (and Thomas had been talking) for about an hour or so. It was no wonder that I pushed him down a steep incline towards the river. It hadn't been meant as an act of aggression. I had only intended to shut him up. However, I must admit that the sight of him tumbling head over heel down the banking did produce a certain amount of satisfaction, even if it was mainly due to the cessation of his infernal rambling. I scrambled down after him and found him lying crumpled by the river, the side of his head caved in on a sharp rock.

My stomach growled.

He provided a far more enjoyable meal than a potential playmate.

When I got home I said that he had wandered off. What remained of him was found washed up downriver a day or so later.

After Thomas, things became so much easier.

The trick was not to kill people too often. That would obviously raise attention to something being afoot. Over the next four years, the woods gained quite a reputation for being a dangerous place to walk. My mother was constantly telling me to watch where I was wandering when I went out on my nature hunts. I was to make sure that I was walking on firm ground or I would slip and fall like so many inexperienced members of the slowly dwindling community seemed to do time and time again.

And dwindling the community was, not just because of my voracious appetite.

Certain folk felt that it was no longer a safe place to be and they began a gradual exodus. One of the ones to leave was my dear father. Just after my sixteenth birthday, I heard raised voices from my parents' room and I went out to sit on the riverbank to enjoy some solitude. When I came back in, he had gone. My mother never explained why; she just moved on.

And so did I.

I decided that the commune was becoming a somewhat awkward place for harvesting my delicious snacks. There were only so many unfortunate accidents that could realistically occur. So, one fine autumn day I ventured out to the nearby city. I had only been there a few times with my mother when we had shopped at an independent workers' co-operative down a small back alley, so it was to this establishment that I headed. I walked inside the shop and made a pretence of examining their organic and wholefood produce, whilst all the time my stomach was rumbling and gurgling, crying out for its desired sustenance. It was late in the day and near to closing time. I could see that the young woman behind the counter was keen to get going. She kept looking at me and then at her watch. She obviously had better places to be than somewhere surrounded by dirty carrots and half-mouldy apples.

I smiled and left the shop, but did not go far. I hid myself just around the corner at the back of the alley and, when she came out to lock the door, I pounced. I slipped one hand over her mouth and, with the other, I drew a keen-edged penknife across her slender throat. I moaned at the smell of the precious blood flowing down her front but I controlled myself and dragged her back into the shop, letting her bleed out and die on the floor as I locked the door shut.

What a feast I had that night! The fresh meat was so tender and delicate.

However, it did bring some rather unwanted attention.

In the past, I had been able to dispatch my food in the woods and let nature give me a helping hand. Here I had no way of disposing of the girl's remains, so I just left them there in the shop — a victim of an everyday passing cannibalistic murderer. There was no way that they could trace it to me, was there?

Living in a commune all my life, I was blissfully unaware of four letters that could spell my doom: CCTV.

In two days' time, my blurred image was all over the local press: a barbaric monster stalking the streets of a fair northern city.

Mother wasn't happy about this.

I tried to explain, I really did. She was my mother, after all — my life-giver. Surely she should understand that my body was just expressing what it desired. There was shouting and screaming. Then screaming of a different kind.

It saddened me that she was probably going to go to waste, but I had to hoof it out of there, so I took her hand to keep me company on the road. It would do as a snack.

Servant of the Lord

It was cold, bitterly cold. As Jacob stared up at the cloudless night, he stamped his feet on the hard ground and slapped his arms around each other in a futile attempt to get warm. The pale, white orb up above just peered down, mockingly.

What I would give for a small hearth right now, he thought to himself. *Just a few glowing embers.*

After adjusting the grubby rags he had manufactured into makeshift gloves, the chilled guard stretched his hands out in front of him. Stretching his fingers and cracking his knuckles, Jacob allowed himself the feeling of a few smouldering pieces of wood to warm the frigid digits, if only in his mind. Developing the illusion, a grin formed on his stubbled face as he wriggled his dirty fingers before the phantasmagorical flames.

A harsh wind swept around the corner of the stone building behind him and he swore loudly, the attempt at imaginary warmth instantly obliterated.

No, there would be no fire here tonight, not a single glowing piece of scrap wood to keep even a single digit from going blue.

Fire and flame were not allowed whilst he was on duty. The only flames that burned nearby were in the brazier in the centre of the temple complex, a reminder to all who saw it of the protection their Lord provided for them.

In an alternative attempt to take his mind off the insidious chill that was creeping through his muscles, Jacob turned his attention to the large doors that he was guarding. Massive wooden affairs, they towered above him. He traced numb fingertips over the rough surface of one of them, feeling the patterns of the wood: the notches and grooves that spoke of the wear of time. They were certainly older than him. Older than his father, gone to ground ten seasons now, even. It was told it had taken twenty trees each to fashion them. The cold guard rubbed his stubbly chin and shook his head. He didn't believe that for an instant. All the trees he knew were spindly, pathetic little things. There was no way that they could have been used to manufacture such large pieces of wood.

No, there had to be another method employed here, and Jacob reckoned he knew what it was.

Magic.

It stood to reason, really. Every soul in the village knew that their Lord was mighty powerful. Some had even felt his power first-hand when they had displeased him. Jacob shuddered at the thought as the memory of charred flesh assaulted his nostrils. Aye, it did not do to offend the Lord. He was quick to anger and slow to forgive, so one should always stay on the right side of a flowing river. No, these doors had been drawn up out of the ground by the Lord himself. He used his powerful magic to fashion them. It was the only way.

Face it, Jacob mused, *He's fashioned other things from the earth*.

Talking of which…

Thud, thud…

The sound of solid footsteps reached the man's ear and he felt his throat go suddenly dry. Turning towards the approaching noise, the guard watched as the giant loomed into the light of the full moon.

He would never find the sight of the Lord's constructs settling. No, not ever. With their tall, featureless bodies and smooth, claylike skin, there was just nothing about them that you could call *natural*.

Magic: he told himself again. *Magic.*

Jacob raised a hand in greeting. "Hello…" His voice came out like a squeaking hinge on a neglected box. Clearing his throat, he tried again. "Hello, friend. Walk you well tonight?"

The construct strode slowly up to the human and paused in front of the smaller creature. It did not say a word. Instead, its long, black tongue slipped out of the slit on its face that it possessed instead of a mouth. The muscular tongue slithered across the space between monster and man and seemed to thoughtfully trace the outline of the guard.

Jacob stood stock still, not wanting to flinch and cause the construct to react, but also not wanting to inadvertently have the tongue touch his skin.

After a short, agonising while, the tongue squirmed back inside the construct's face and the creature, seemingly satisfied, turned and continued its patrol of the perimeter.

Jacob watched it disappear around the corner of the building that they both guarded and, only when it was out of sight, did he allow himself a breath. By the Dragon, those things were terrifying! He knew that they were there

27

for everyone's protection, but still…

Something about them was completely unsettling. Something deep down inside his head screamed for him to run every time he saw one of them or one of the Shadow Wraiths. The guard shuddered once more. The Wraiths were even worse! They disturbed him more than a sudden downpour did the surface of a puddle. They looked more human than the normal constructs, having recognisable features such as eyes, a nose and a mouth but, again, they were just *wrong*. It was as if someone had tried to create a human being and had just not been able to get it quite right. Something was missing. Was it something in their cold stare? Perhaps it was the way that their hair did not move at all, slick against their scalp? Jacob wasn't sure. All he knew was that they deeply troubled him.

He was just glad that, like the other constructs, the Wraiths were there to protect those who served the Lord.

Unlike the unfortunates that had been carted through these doors earlier on.

Jacob blew on his fingers as he recalled the scene from just before the sun's setting. He had only been on duty a short while when a Shadow Wraith had ridden up on its horse, three constructs marching in its wake. Two of the clay soldiers had each been carrying an unconscious human in their arms. Jacob hadn't wanted to stare as that could have gotten him into bother, but he had snuck a quick peek at the two that had been dead to the world. They had been a man and a lad. The fellow had been about his age and the boy certainly less than two decades, he had reckoned. The boy looked like he had seen a hard time. His clothes were ripped and wet; there were scorch marks on his skin. The man had just been like a snuffed-out candle. The curious thing was their clothing. It was unlike anything that he had seen before. It certainly didn't look practical. It was far too lightweight, by the looks of it. Brightly coloured too. You certainly couldn't blend in whilst wearing it. No good for hunting down a meal, that was for sure.

One thing Jacob was sure of, they weren't local. He would have recognised them if they had been. He pondered the possibility that they were from some far-off village, somewhere not under the protection of the Lord. That made sense. Most likely they had heard of the great things that the subjects of the Lord possessed and they had come to try and steal them. The Wraith and the constructs had stopped them.

That was what they did.

They protected the servants of the Lord.

Jacob started.

Had he just heard something?

He peered out into the vast, moonlit gloom and saw nothing. Shrugging to himself, he dismissed it. It was just the thought of others out there wanting the good things that he and his kin had. *Let's face it*, he thought to himself, *no one would be stupid enough to attack the Temple of the Lord!* No, with its massive stone walls and these huge doors, there was no way that anyone could ever get in. It was a stronghold, safe and sure.

Plus, there were the constructs: unstoppable, incorruptible, deadly.

Sure, you heard things. There were tales that reached the village of foolish folk who thought that they had it bad. Jacob grunted to himself. What more could folk want than a roof over their head and food in their belly? Sure, it might not be *much* food and there was always that background rumble in the guts, but times were hard, weren't they? They knew that because the Lord told them so, and he would know because he was… well… all-knowing.

No, there were stories, for sure, but they made as much sense as that lad who'd had six fingers on one hand and had drooled all the time before drowning in a puddle. Some folk just liked to gossip. They talked about a special man who was going to save them all.

Save them?

From what?

They were all perfectly safe. The Lord saw to that; the Lord and his constructs.

Jacob started again. There had definitely been something that time. It had been a cracking of a twig or something similar. He grabbed his knife from his belt and thrust it out in front of him. "Who walks by?" he shouted into the dark. "Who walks by?"

The darkness failed to reply.

The guard's head snapped from side to side trying to discern any movement in the moonlight, but all he could make out were shadows stretching out into the night. His tongue slipped across his lips which he then bit down upon as he tightened his grip around his knife.

"I suggest you drop that ridiculous piece of metal and walk away."

The man almost jumped out of his skin at the sound of the female voice next to his ear. He spun around and backed away in one floundering lurch. He yelled out in pain as sharp fingers clenched his wrist, causing him to drop his knife. The grasp on his wrist twisted and he found himself rump to the floor, gawping up at his attacker.

A girl.

Jacob frowned. "Who are you? What are you doing here?"

The girl was in her mid-teens, wearing a long dark cloak that covered what seemed to be chestnut brown hair. She rolled her eyes and said, "I told you to leave. Now leave."

Jacob looked around. There was no one else in sight. Feeling slightly braver now he knew it was just a girl, he dragged himself up from the dirt and rounded on his attacker. "Don't you tell me what to do, girlie! You run off home to your mother and we'll forget this ever happened."

The girl just shook her head before her gaze shot towards the corner of the Temple.

A familiar two-beat tread caused the ground to shake.

"Oh, you're in trouble now, girlie," Jacob grinned. "Just you wait and see."

The construct rounded the corner and did not break stride as it homed in on the intruder.

The girl did not run.

The girl did not cower in fear.

The girl did not beg for mercy.

She smiled.

There was the sound of wet clay being remoulded and the construct's three-fingered arm became a sharp lance held up menacingly towards the youth.

The girl seemed to mimic the creature as she also held out a hand. A look of concentration crossed her face and she seemed to push at the air in front of her with her fingers. A green mist was expelled from her hand and enveloped the deadly golem.

The construct became nothing but dust on the currents of the air.

Jacob screamed out and dove for his knife. He snatched it up and swung it towards the girl who was now advancing on him. "Stay back!" he screamed. "Stay back! The Lord will stop you!"

There was a sharp sensation of pain as the girl's booted foot kicked his knife out of his grip. This was followed by a confusing flurry of movement as she leapt behind him. The last thing Jacob felt was the firm grip of her hands on the sides of his head. For a brief moment, the world looked as if it had been turned over on a peculiar angle.

Then there was nothing.

Craft

As the grasping fingers of the wintry gale clawed their way through the ill-maintained house, Ethel pulled the hand-stitched quilt up to her chin, content with the knowledge that her shiftless late husband was now at least providing some adequate service in the bedroom.

Mother and Son

It was dark.

But then, it always was, wasn't it? That was sort of the lot of a vampire, one of the *children of the night...* Nightingale suppressed a chuckle as she heard the words roll around her head in a dreadful impersonation of Bela Lugosi.

"You okay?"

The petite vampire just smiled as she turned her head to regard her companion, a sandy-haired man who appeared to be, and indeed actually was, in his mid-thirties. She studied his kind features and his currently furrowed brow. "I'm good, Dave," she reassured her son. "Mind just wandering, that's all."

The man nodded and shifted position slightly. He looked back down from their vantage point into the narrow alley below, wincing as he did so.

"Cramp?" Nightingale asked.

He nodded. "I thought it was something that wasn't supposed to affect us."

"If you get any creature to lie flat on a roof for four hours, I guess most of them will eventually become uncomfortable. Where is it?"

"My right leg. Damn thing's gone dead."

"It's been dead ever since that car hit you."

The man turned back to face her. "Vampire humour?"

"Vampire humour," she grinned, her blue eyes twinkling mischievously.

The male chuckled to himself and wriggled slightly, trying to awaken the sleeping limb.

"Any good?"

"A bit. Still not as tortuous as four hours in a car with the Potency."

Nightingale raised an eyebrow. "I can imagine. I guess the little rock was slightly over-excited."

The male just snorted in amusement.

"Well, at least you're having some quality mother-and-son time now. Far more relaxing."

"Tell that to my leg," Dave smiled.

His mother smiled back.

"What?"

"Nothing," Nightingale shrugged.

"No, it's not *nothing*. What's up?"

The female vampire chuckled. "It's silly."

"Then I definitely want to know what it is. It'll take my mind off my dead leg."

"I was just thinking about how I'm so proud of you."

"You're right," Dave snorted. "It's silly."

Nightingale shook her head. "No… no, it's not. Not really. You've come from such a different background to most of us and you've just sort of fitted in so well. You had a normal life that was snatched away from you, yet you don't complain about your lot. It's not all *woe is me!*"

The younger vampire shrugged. "What would it

achieve?"

"Exactly. That's just what I mean. You're so prag-matic. So stoic. You had a nice little life in Lancaster, selling your comics and whatever else it was you had in that little shop. Now… now you're on top of a rooftop in the middle of the night waiting to ambush a clay killing machine. And you don't whinge or whine one little bit."

"No one else complains about being a vampire. Take Tigress and Scorp: they revel in it."

"That's because their human lives were awful af-fairs, as were those of most of us. Tigress was the daugh-ter of an overbearing chief; Scorpion was in a toxic rela-tionship with a fallen angel in a doomed city; I was no more than a slave to a sadistic parish priest. We wanted to escape our lives and being turned into vamps gave us a rope of knotted sheets with which to flee our prison cell."

Dave shrugged. "I guess."

"It changed us physically and emotionally." Nightin-gale let her blue eyes wander over the face of her son. "You, however, are still… *you*. Do you think that's why you haven't taken a new name yet?"

The younger vampire groaned. "Not this again."

"Dave, it's tradition. When we are born anew, we take a new name that represents what we truly are. Mine came from my singing voice that drew my father to me and Marcus took his name from Marcus Aurelius because of his love for philosophy."

"What about Tigress and Scorpion?"

"I've never had the opportunity to ask them."

"Scorp I can understand. There will have been scorpions where she grew up and she certainly has a sting in her tail. Tigress, though… She grew up in Neo-lithic Britain. How the hell did she know about a big cat from India?"

"Perhaps it was a sabre tooth tiger? Were they still around in her time?"

Dave's head waggled from side to side. "Could be, I guess."

"So?"

"So what?"

"Your name. Any candidates?"

"No," came the quick response.

Nightingale's eyes twinkled. "Now, why don't I believe you?"

Her son shifted awkwardly on the rooftop.

"Come on, out with it."

"There's nothing. Honest."

"Liar." The young woman tapped her finger against her smile. "It's from one of your comic books, isn't it? That's why you don't want to tell me."

Her son's silence confirmed her suspicions.

"Oooo... Let me guess..."

"Please don't. It's embarrassing."

"Is it the beefcake with the hammer?"

"No. Not Thor."

"What about that blind guy in red?"

"Daredevil? No."

"Hmmm... Let's see... There's that fellow with the bow and arrow."

"Hawkeye? Nah. The TV series put me off that one."

"But you considered it?"

Dave shrugged and quickly changed the subject. "So, you really think Asmodeus is here? You think he's looking for our little green friend?"

Nightingale grimaced. "He sees the Potency as his

property. He did create it, after all. After Lucifer split it, he stashed away the half that we encountered in Lancaster. If he has any inkling as to where you hid it, he's going to come running."

"But how would he know? We didn't even tell Sam where we were taking it."

"The Fallen wouldn't dare approach Spallucci again. Your friend bested and humiliated him." Nightingale peered down into the alleyway below. "No. He'll be trying other ways to track down his little rock of devastation."

"What do you think those might be?"

"I don't know and that worries me." Somewhere in the distance, a church clock chimed the hour. "Marcus is taking his time. He should be here by now." She rolled over onto her back and gazed up at the sky. "So, how's things?"

"I think there's a modicum of sensation creeping back into my leg."

"That's not what I meant."

The male vampire stared resolutely down into the dark alley.

"Dave?"

"What?"

"You fell asleep in the car on the way down here."

"So?"

"We don't normally sleep. We don't need it."

"I guess the last few days have been over-tiring," the male shrugged. "In vampire terms, I'm still young. A mere babe in arms," he grinned disarmingly.

"It wasn't a restful little nap. You were dreaming."

"Oh. Was I drooling too? That would be gross."

A small smile touched Nightingale's lips. "No, you

weren't." She rolled back onto her side and her blue eyes fixed on her son. "Want to talk about it?"

Dave sighed. "Do I have to?"

"I'm your mother. Humour me."

The male vampire shifted to face his mother, wincing at the pins and needles in his leg. "It's not much. It was just an image really."

"An image? Of a place?"

He shook his head.

"A person?"

"It was a woman. A young one, probably about your age."

Nightingale raised an eyebrow. "A hundred and forty? She must have been well preserved."

"No," Dave chuckled. "Your age when you became a vampire. Early twenties."

"Someone you know?"

He shook his head. "Never seen her before in my life. Long, chestnut brown hair. Brown eyes."

"Sounds quite the catch."

A vague blush appeared on the male vampire's cheeks. "It wasn't *that* sort of dream. You really think I'd be talking to my mother about it if it was?"

"Good point. So what else can you tell me about this adorable-looking woman?"

"Not much, really. I just knew I had to find her."

"Any idea where she is?"

The male vampire hesitated.

"What is it?"

"I... don't think she's in these parts yet. I think she's from the future."

His mother's eyes narrowed. "How *far* in the future?"

Dave swallowed nervously. "I have the feeling it was post-Divergence. There was nothing there to explicitly say it was… It just *felt* like it. You got any explanation?"

The female vampire seemed to idly doodle in the dirt on the rooftop with her fingertip as she pondered what her son had just described. Eventually, she said, "I do, and it's big and watery."

"The Abyss?"

Nightingale nodded. "When you dropped off her offspring, the Potency, the Abyss took you and the others post-Divergence, didn't she?"

"Yes. Only briefly. I'm not sure if she *physically* took us or just showed us something."

"What was it?"

"A boy and a girl in the distance, walking through the Divergent Lands, talking to each other."

"Did you see their faces?"

He shook his head. "It was very brief. I don't think I'd recognise them again."

Nightingale sighed. "The Abyss doesn't do anything without a very good reason. Hell, she destroyed the roof and the insides of All Saints church just to reach out to me when I was there. I reckon she's left an imprint of this woman in your mind."

"How?"

"She's an omniscient sentient ocean that has existed from the beginning of time. I'm sure she has her ways."

"Good point." Dave paused. "So, why?"

"Again, she's an omniscient sentient ocean that has existed from the beginning of time," Nightingale frowned. "To her, we are just little ants to play with on a stick. I don't think we can begin to fathom her reasons."

"Again, good point."

A silence fell between the two vampires.

Nightingale checked her watch.

Dave fiddled with a loose piece of slate on the roof.

"What was it like?" the son eventually asked his mother. "When the Abyss sang in the church."

"Wet," Nightingale replied. "Very wet." She grimaced. "Seriously, though, it was unlike anything else I've ever experienced. Words simply can't do it justice. It was raw, primordial power sweeping through the building. I lay there in the nave of the church, curled up like a small babe, as the waters flooded up from under the font.

"I should have been afraid, terrified.

"But, I wasn't.

"It's song consumed me and it was the most beautiful thing that I've ever heard." Nightingale smiled to herself. "It took a hell of a lot of work to repair the church." She reached into an inside pocket of her jacket and fished something out. "Here. Look at this."

Dave took what he was offered: a small, white envelope. He pulled out a sepia-coloured photograph that showed a group of people standing around a stone font. "This is All Saints, after the installation of the font."

Nightingale nodded.

"It hasn't changed a bit," Dave mused. He pointed to a stick-thin maid at the edge of the photograph. "That's you, isn't it?"

"My last photograph as a human. I was, quite literally, at death's door."

"Who are the others?"

"That," Nightingale pointed to a severe-looking priest, "was my sadistic employer. Those," she motioned to a number of other individuals, "were important members of the parish."

Dave's finger rested on the last two members of the image. "What about these two?"

"Those are the ones responsible for the renovations to the church. They single-handedly motivated the wealthy members of the parish to fork out and get it fixed. I seem to recall it only took a week or so. Quite the mammoth undertaking." She made to say more when there was a sudden commotion down below. "Well, it looks like our waiting is over. Here comes Marcus with a friend."

They peered down over the parapet and watched as the grey-haired vampire pursued someone down into the back street. Nightingale and Dave both inhaled deeply and grimaced.

"Construct," the male vampire growled.

Nightingale rose to her feet. "Well, we'd better go and help out. Marcus will only grumble if we don't." With that, she leapt lightly down into the dark alley.

Dave made to follow and realised that he still held the photograph. He slipped it back into its envelope and placed it carefully in a coat pocket. He would give it back to his mother later. Then, he too, jumped down into the fray.

It was a teenage girl. Well, it *looked* like a teenage girl. Dave reminded himself that constructs, clay-based shapeshifters, were insanely good at hiding in plain sight. They were all over the globe, posing as normal humans and waiting for the day that Kanor would flick their switch and activate them, bringing about the Divergence, the fall of humanity. Until then, the majority of the deadly sleeper agents went about their mundane lives, completely oblivious to the fact that their sole existence was the near genocide of the alpha species of the planet.

In short, none of them had a clue as to their true nature.

Just like the terrified girl in front of the three strangers who had her trapped in a dark alley.

"Please," she wailed, her voice tremulous, "don't hurt me." The blonde-haired girl backed further into the alley and stumbled as her leg knocked over a broken wooden crate. "Please, please let me go. I won't tell anyone."

The young vampire's shoulders rose and fell as his body instinctively produced a simulacrum of a sigh. As they did, his nose caught a whiff of something vile, something dank. Yes, the constructs may look and behave like humans, but their noxious stench always gave them away. He remembered when his mother had taken him on his first hunt. It had been an utter disaster! His mortal emotions had baulked at stalking and killing something that looked like a human. If it hadn't been for the intervention of Nightingale's tall, grey-haired companion, his own journey as a Child of Cain would have been cut short after just a few days.

The creature in front of them appeared to be a young human, scared to death of the strangers advancing on her. In reality, it was an obscenity that could strike all three of its attackers down in an instant. True, all three of them knew how they were supposed to die — they had each seen it in their birth dreams. However, life had a funny way of rolling loaded dice, so it was always best to be careful.

Besides, being stabbed by a construct's lance would hurt like a bitch, even if it wasn't fatal.

As the creature that looked like a fragile young girl

continued to whimper, the three Children of Cain ex-
changed silent glances before their movements became
a blur. The girl screamed as she flew through the air,
slamming soundly into the wall of the alley, Marcus pinning her immobile. She cried for help as Dave ripped
open her clothing, exposing a smooth stomach devoid of
a navel — the other sign that the thing in front of them
wasn't human. The creature fell silent as Nightingale produced a sharp knife which the vampire began to dig into
the soft material that posed as flesh on the creature's
chest.

Then all hell broke loose.

Close to where the knife jutted out of the construct's chest, a wicked lance erupted through the torn
blouse. Nightingale swore and just managed to dodge
more or less out of the way as the deadly weapon grazed
her cheek. Dave felt himself tumbling backwards as the
construct's right leg twisted round at a peculiar angle and
caught him in the stomach. Marcus cried out as the
shoulders that he was pinning to the wall sunk in on themselves, allowing the creature to slide down and out of his
grasp.

The vampires recovered and regrouped, throwing
themselves at the now fully aware, fully awake construct.
What lurched along the shadows of the alley could now
not be described as at all human. Its body was a contorted and twisted mass of misshapen limbs, its head
cocked over on one side above the fallen shoulders. The
chimera hissed as the vampires roughly grabbed it and
cast it back into the depths of the alley. It thrashed wildly
as they pinned it down once more, this time on the de-
tritus-strewn floor. It bucked and shook, thrusting more
lances up from its chest, all of which were nimbly avoided

by its attackers. Its arms extended out beyond any human length. The claw-like hand of one grabbed Marcus by the scruff of the neck and pulled him away, dangling the vampire like a puppet on a string; the fingers on the other limb moulded together and formed a wicked-looking lance that it stabbed wildly at the other two vampires.

"Enough!" screamed Nightingale as she once more thrust the knife down into the construct's chest. The monster's face twisted, the features momentarily losing cohesion before snapping back to those of the young girl. It screamed in agony as the vampire twisted the knife ninety degrees. It dropped Marcus and its other arm fell flat to the ground. The creature of clay tried to push itself up from the floor of the alleyway but Nightingale twisted the knife once more and it finally fell silent, defeated.

The construct blinked and a pair of white, lifeless orbs peered up at the female vampire. "As I fall, others shall rise," came its voice, no longer that of a terrified young human, but the wet, ragged sounds of a creature that was fashioned for murder, not conversation.

"Of that, I have no doubt," Nightingale agreed, pushing her dark hair back with her free hand. She ran a finger over her wounded cheek and felt the scratch from the construct heal shut as she kept a tight hold on the knife with her other hand. "And we will destroy them all."

A wet gurgle erupted from the mouth of the construct as its mouth widened up to its ears. "No, little leech, you will not. You will fail. You will die. You will *all* die." Its white pupil-less eyes held the Queen of the Children of Cain. "*He* has seen it!"

"Asmodeus?" Marcus snorted in contempt. "From what I've heard, the Fallen can't see the backs of his hands when they're in front of his face in a well-lit room."

The construct emitted another wet gurgle of derision. "That is not who I mean… The Black Dragon knows all, sees all. He is far greater than the sum of the parts of your pitiful little cadre. He has obtained mastery over time and space. He has seen you fall, all one after the other. One," it glared at Marcus, "in the light of day. One," it turned its head to Nightingale, "at the sound of a gunshot fired by the one you seek this very night. The other," it moved its attention to the youngest vampire and chuckled once again, "in the very presence of the Black Dragon himself. No, Kanor will outlive you all. What you do to me or my kindred will not affect that.

"You cannot stop him.

"It is preordained."

The construct's inhuman laugh contorted into a wet scream as Nightingale twisted the blade even further. "It doesn't matter what fate holds for us," she snapped. "We will continue to do our duty. Like stopping the Fallen from getting his grubby mitts on the Potency.

"Where is he?"

The construct began to breathe deeply, composing itself to ride the waves of pain. As it did so, a thick, black tongue lolled out of the wide gash that had replaced its mouth. Like a cobra rising from a charmer's basket, the tongue danced up in front of the three vampires in turn, before retracting back into the distorted features of the monster that lay impaled on the floor.

"Why should I tell you? You will kill me, anyway. Just as you do all my kindred."

Nightingale's face hardened and she twisted the knife once again. "Slow and painful or quick and merciful. Your choice."

Bubbles erupted from the construct's over-wide

mouth as it fought the agonising torture. "Merciful? Merciful? When are your kind ever merciful? You know nothing of the sort. You are obsessed with your three little tasks and precious little else. You would sacrifice anything to fulfil the tenets of Cain." Its white eyes swivelled over to Dave and back to Nightingale. "Or any*one*."

"What the hell do you mean by that?" Nightingale hissed.

"My dear *Queen*," the construct spat, "you will leave your son alone to wander the Divergent Lands. He will have no hope, no purpose save the last remaining instruction that burns in his heart. It will consume him and lead him to his death at the hands of the Black Dragon.

"All because you weren't there to guide him.

"All because you abandoned him at such a young, delicate age."

The golem screamed in agony as Nightingale rammed the knife deeper inside and up into its chest cavity. "Slow and painful it is, then," the vampire growled.

"A farmstead!" the construct cried out. "A farmstead! It's to the north of here, three miles out from the edge of town. It's the first of its kind along the road. You cannot miss it. You will find the Fallen there." The construct's eyelids closed over the lifeless orbs and they melted into its waxy skin.

Nightingale looked over at Marcus and nodded. As one they fell upon the deadly creature and drained it dry.

"You do know it's a trap, don't you?"

Nightingale dusted the remains of the clay creature off her short leather jacket and turned to face her son. "That doesn't mean we should ignore the possibility that Asmodeus is where the creature said he is. We have to stop him before he finds the Potency. Should he lay his hands on that little green rock…" Her voice trailed off and she shuddered.

"Do you think it was telling the truth? Not about the location of the Fallen, but that he's the one who will kill you?"

The female vampire blew the final speck of dust off her sleeve. "My child, we all know how we will die. We have seen it when we were reborn. I already know that I will die at the hands of someone with a gun. If it's a pompous oaf with a god complex, well, that's somewhat embarrassing, but there's nothing that I can do about it."

Dave screwed his face up in thought. "Sam should have killed him when he had the chance."

Nightingale's hand flew to her son's arm and she shook her head. "No. Not at all. What Sam Spallucci did… Dave, he created a construct to do his bidding. He acted in pure anger, seeking out revenge. If he had killed someone, it would have tipped him over the edge. Pray your friend never has to take a life. There's no coming back from that. Not ever."

"He's already taken out at least one werewolf."

"That was self-defence, not premeditated." Nightingale gave her child's arm a gentle squeeze before turning to face her longtime companion. "So, onward and upward?"

Marcus nodded. "As always. As we must."

Nightingale smiled and said to her son, "Go back to the others. Tell them what has happened here and that we are heading to engage Asmodeus."

"Wait. You're not taking me with you? Surely we can just ring them?"

His mother reached up and stroked his cold cheek.

Hear My Scare

"This is not your path, my son. The others will need you, should we not return. Promise me you will guide them."

Dave could not speak. He just nodded and then watched as his mother and her companion ran off into the night. Silently, in the darkness of a dirty alleyway, he rubbed a single tear of blood from his cheek. Thrusting his hands into his coat pockets, he felt the envelope that contained the photo of his mother.

Lessons Learned

A bright full moon hung silently in the sky, passively observing all that was unfolding down below.

A teenage girl stood on her own and stared up at the curious patterns that covered the white disk. Her sharp, youthful eyesight tracked along spiderwebs that seemed to emanate from round nests dotted at random points upon its surface. She wondered whether the irregular dark splodges were land masses, or perhaps they were ancient seas upon which people had sailed space boats thousands of years ago.

She knew that in the days before the Divergence, people had reached the cold rock that floated in the night sky, so they must have done *something* up there when they reached it. What would have been the point of going so far just to sit on a rock for a bit before coming home?

They had been brave adventurers, travelling out into the unknown, leaving the familiarity of the hearth long behind them.

Just as she had done.

She felt a sigh over her shoulder.

"You know I don't like it when you judge me," she

snapped without turning around. "I did the right thing."

Again the sigh.

Reluctantly and with great hesitation, the girl turned around. She saw him, as she always did: just a bit younger than she was now; the same age as he had been when he left her. His brown eyes regarded her from under his messy hair.

Did you, Katy? the eyes questioned her. *Did you really do the right thing?*

"Yes!" the girl snapped to the air in front of her. "I did! Don't you dare to question me! You left me! Abandoned me when you rode out on your stupid quest. She took me in and cared for me.

"She," the girl flexed her fingers, "made me stronger."

The apparition of her brother shook its head. *Dad would not approve.*

"Our father was weak. That weakness got him killed."

The memory just sighed and faded away.

Katy snorted in contempt and turned towards the task at hand. First, she settled her two horses. An infiltration of the temple complex and the rescue of those inside would be for nothing if her means of escape were discovered. Running her hand over the firm, bristly cheeks of the large beasts, she muttered in a low, carefully precise voice the strange words that she had been taught.

"They sound funny," she had complained as she had initially struggled to wrap her teeth and her tongue around them.

Her teacher had arched a perfect eyebrow in amusement. "That is because they are in a very ancient language," the woman had explained. "It hasn't been spoken by humans in well over three millennia."

Katy had rolled her eyes. "Why can't we say them in *our* language? Surely that would be so much easier!"

"It's not just the words. It's the patterns that they form. Everything is about patterns, Katy. The words we say; the arrangement of thoughts in our minds; the unfurling of events throughout history. They all have *purpose.*"

Katy huffed in annoyance. "A purpose designed to cause my head to ache."

Now, though, she whispered the words with accuracy and perfection. As the syllables slid from her tongue, she watched the patterns of the letters forming in her mind, each one glowing with bright luminescence as it was incanted. The horses responded as intended: they stamped their feet, swayed their heads from side to side and gently closed their dark eyelids. The girl stepped back and nodded in satisfaction. The steeds were quiet and immobile, slumbering lightly as they stood. They would make no noise, no braying or whinnying, and would not attract the attention of a passing villager from the nearby pittance of a settlement or a guard from the complex itself.

After quickly and methodically running through her checklist of garb and weapons, Katy set off for her destination.

Katy could easily pick her way through the darkness to the temple complex. The light of the full moon meant that she was able to see exactly where she was going and would not make a fool of herself by tripping over a treacherous stone or root. However, the guiding light was somewhat of a double-edged sword. The land surrounding the complex was open and barren. The so-called *Lord* (Katy gave an impromptu eye roll at the vainglorious title) had commanded that all wood be continually harvested so that a pyre could remain lit upon a large brazier in the centre of the compound: a reminder to his worshippers of the warmth and care that he showered upon them.

A tut of disgust rolled off the girl's lips. She had seen the *warmth and care* that the Fallen had bestowed upon his subjects when she had passed the nearby village. The paths were rutted, the houses were falling down and the residents were malnourished.

It reminded her of her childhood.

Now, however, she resided in a grand palace. She was clean, washed and ate the finest foods. And it had been *her* decision. She had chosen to be strong, to rise up out of the mire and surround herself with a better life.

A life that had brought her on this mission, picking her way through an open landscape as a treacherous lunar light shone down upon her, threatening to betray any mistake or slip-up.

Under her dark cloak, she placed her hands on her hips and considered the situation. The temple complex was within sight which meant that she herself would, obviously, be in sight of any guards that could be bothered to stay awake. Scanning the walls, she saw no immediate sign of movement, but that didn't mean that there wasn't anyone around to raise an alarm or hurl a pathetic excuse for a weapon. Katy screwed her lips in annoyance but cleared her mind of all intrusive thoughts. In the blank space that she formed inside her head, the teenage girl pictured the land around her. In its midst, where she was currently standing, she imagined a veil of grey falling from the night sky to the hard ground. A creeping chill spread across her skin, causing goosebumps to form.

Shivering slightly, she set off towards the temple complex.

She had gone just five paces when she heard a familiar dread sound.

Thud, thud.

Thud, thud.

Katy froze where she stood, a statue immobile in the night. What's more, if the spell broke, she would be a very *visible* statue in the night. As the construct lumbered into view, she breathed slowly, calming her racing heart and concentrating on keeping herself grey, unnoticeable.

"The creations of Kanor," her teacher had instructed her, "are simple creatures. They have one mission: to kill that which stands in their way. If you are not perceived as a threat, then they will ignore you."

"So this spell makes me invisible? They won't see me?"

They had been walking casually down a busy street. All around them, traders were plying their ragged wares to half-starved shoppers. None of them had seen the superior duo passing by.

The teacher shook her head, causing her long, dark hair to brush against her fine cheeks. "No. Invisibility is a treacherous skill. It can easily betray you. You walk across wet grass, you leave footprints behind. You sneak into a sauna to watch some muscular beau relaxing, the steam will swirl around you and reveal your presence. No, you must become *grey*, unnoticeable. You need to take yourself to a state where you are of no concern to those around you. You are just part of the background. It must be as if you have always been there and are of no consequence."

Hear My Scare

As Katy pondered what a *beau* actually was (perhaps it was some sort of ox?) the construct paused midway along its path in front of the tall wall that belonged to the temple complex and gazed out across the barren grassland. Well, it would have gazed, had it owned a pair of eyes. Instead, it opened the gash across its face that acted as a mouth and its long, black tongue slithered out from within. Katy swallowed nervously as the tongue began to sway back and forth. The golem was scenting the air.

I am grey: she thought to herself. *I am of no consequence.* She focused her mind and concentrated on feeling the chill that washed over her skin. She could remove the threat of the construct quite easily, but stealth was the superior weapon.

The construct took two solid footsteps forward.

Katy felt her hand twitch.

The construct stamped slowly onto the grassland.

Katy felt her fingers begin to itch. She willed them to calm down, to remain grey. She wasn't going to use that gift just yet. It was her fallback plan.

The construct paused just over two arms-length in front of her. Its muscular tongue undulated over the air in front of the teenage girl, flickering a mere handspan in front of her nose. Part of her wanted to run; another part wanted to freeze completely. But neither would be a good idea.

"When you encounter your enemy and you wish to remain hidden, you should continue to be yourself. Just, be yourself, more *quietly*," her teacher had explained.

So, as the searching tongue flickered from side to side, threatening to discover the human in front of it, Katy neither bolted nor held her breath. Instead, she washed herself with calm and felt her racing heartbeat slow. She pursed her lips and breathed lightly, rhythmically. She was quite... normal.

The construct's tongue slipped back into its head before the clay beast turned and marched back to the complex where it turned at a sharp angle to resume its patrol of the perimeter.

Katy grinned and headed up to the wall.

This was her next obstacle.

The stone wall was a sheer height that towered above her. Her mistress' palace was a large structure, but it was welcoming and was a place of beauty. It mirrored the woman that dwelt within. Its columns and colonnades were engraved with flowing symbols and images of nature. Water trickled peacefully in the sanctuary and acolytes lounged in peaceful bliss. This building performed a likewise task of symbolising its own occupant. Stark and fortified, it spoke of power and dominance. It was designed to keep intruders out, apart from the dweller within. It marked a line in the dirt across which the plebs were not allowed to cross on pain of death. Most likely a brutal and excruciating one at that.

Katy placed her hands on her hips and grimaced as she saw no possible handholds or cracks in the mortar that would aid an ascent.

"It is a fool who expends more energy into a task at hand than is absolutely necessary," her teacher had instructed her time and time again. "You will never know when you will need to draw upon your deep reserves for an unexpected task. Always conserve your energy whenever possible. Take time to seek out the simplest way to perform what might appear to be an overwhelming task."

Hear My Scare

Katy sighed and looked along the sheer wall to the corner from around which the construct had appeared.

The front door it was, then.

There was a guard. Just the one. At a guess, the Fallen that dwelt in this temple complex did not see humans as a serious threat. His blind ego dictated that they worshipped him as a god so they would never dare to breach his defences.

What need would they have to do so?

But times were changing.

"Never underestimate the general populace," her teacher had warned her. "Yes, Kanor reduced them to a pitiful remnant, purging all their decadence and hubris from the planet, but all it takes is one spark to kindle a fire."

"You're talking of the Virtuous Man," Katy had replied.

A shadow had fallen across her teacher's face. "Perhaps. Perhaps not. The future is a fickle thing, my child. Never assume that those you know will play the part that is written for them."

So, not wanting to underestimate the one pitiful guard who stood shivering in the cold night, Katy kept herself grey and approached as quietly as possible until she found herself standing next to him. She could easily slip by, that was for sure. His mind was obviously focused more on the chill that was wracking his skinny form through his tattered rags than it was on keeping watch. However, she would not be on her own coming back and there was no way of knowing how those she had been sent to rescue would be able to handle themselves. If they had suffered at the hands of the Fallen in the way that her teacher suspected then they would not be up to making a quick dash out of the gate.

Which meant that the guard had to be removed from the escape route.

She took a careful step forward.

The guard started and Katy paused. He was a nervous soul, this one, jumping at shadows. She watched as he peered out in front of him into the gloom that stretched out before the main gate. Smiling, she bent and picked up a small pebble, then threw it against the wall. The poor guard stifled a scream and spun around, drawing a pathetic excuse for a dagger from the narrow belt that held up his trousers. "Who walks by?" his trembling voice yelled into the dark. "Who walks by?"

As the guard's head snapped from side to side in a vain attempt to locate the source of the noise, Katy strode confidently to his side and said, "I suggest you drop that ridiculous piece of metal and walk away."

The man shrieked in fear and waved the knife blindly to his side. Katy grimaced and bent out of the way. It would be embarrassing to be nicked by such a useless implement. She reached out and grabbed the wrist of the hand that held the knife. Forcing her fingers in deep against his tendons, she caused the man to simultaneously yell out in pain and drop the pathetic excuse for a weapon. Twisting her grip, she yanked him around and decentralised his centre of balance, causing him to fall rear-first onto the floor.

The man gawped up at her in disbelief as she let the greyness fall away. "Who are you? What are you doing here?" he yammered.

Katy didn't have time for questions. Impatiently, she rolled her eyes and snapped, "I told you to leave. Now leave."

The guard peered around his attacker. Seeing that she was alone, he rather foolishly recovered some bravado. Using the wall behind him, he pulled himself up to his feet, straightened his clothing and rounded on the solitary teenage girl who only came up to his chin. "Don't you tell me what to do, girlie! You run off home to your mother and we'll forget this ever happened."

Why are people so stupid? Katy asked herself. She shook her head and was about to lash out with a simple disabling blow when a familiar noise reached her ears as the ground beneath her feet trembled.

"Oh, you're in trouble now, girlie," the guard grinned wickedly. "Just you wait and see."

The construct rounded the corner and did not break stride as it homed in on the intruder.

Katy did not run.

Katy did not cower in fear.

Katy did not beg for mercy.

She smiled.

All need for stealth was now gone. She felt the warmth start to flow into her fingers as the killing machine moulded its three-fingered arm into a lance.

As Katy held out her hand, she recalled the day that her teacher had said, "It wasn't Kanor who created the first constructs you know. It was me.

"I also know how to destroy them."

The memory of a small girl with green hair and glowing eyes touching her temples blossomed in Katy's memory and she felt the heat in her fingertips intensify. She felt the purest power from the small girl build inside her head and surge down through her arm. She watched in fascination as the force erupted from her fingertips in the form of a green mist. The mist paused as if it was deciding its next move and then, sensing the advancing construct, it rushed forward and enveloped the clay creature.

In an instant, the monster was nothing but motes of dust in the air.

Katy was aware that the guard was screaming but his terror was nothing compared to the exhilaration that now filled her body. She lifted her hand to her face and her wide brown eyes studied her fingertips as the green mist danced delicately around her nails before it sank back into her skin.

The power… It was amazing!

She heard the sound of metal scraping on stone as the guard snatched up his knife. "Stay back!" he screamed as Katy stalked towards the pathetic creature that stood in her way. "Stay back! The Lord will stop you!"

In a swift, graceful movement, she kicked the knife out of the man's hand and jumped up over him, landing deftly in his blind spot. Grabbing the sides of his head in her hands, she twisted and the guard fell lifeless to the floor.

Katy closed her eyes and revelled in the carnage.

In the darkness of her head, she replayed over and over again the image of the construct becoming dust.

Opening her eyes, she saw the spirit of her brother standing in front of the main gate, his face pure sorrow.

Katy strode past him into the temple complex.

Nothing could stop her now.

Bubbles

"So, this is where we aerate the mixture."

The detective pretended to scribble something in his battered notebook before rolling his neck around on his tired shoulders. His leaden footsteps felt laboured on the metal catwalk above the vats of sickly sweet brown gloop that were currently being stirred by some sort of large paddle mechanism. The swirling and undulating mixture cruelly mimicked the roiling sensation in his unsettled stomach. He flicked his eyes in what he hoped was a surreptitious manner to the clock that hung suspended on the wall of the cavernous room.

An hour! Dear God, he'd been here an hour already!

The detective ran the back of his hand over his clammy forehead. "And this is where the theft occurred?" He seriously hoped it was. He'd already been dragged around far too many rooms to count in the supersized chocolate factory. Last night had been a heavy one. He just wanted to escape to the comfort of a padded office chair where he could gently lie his head down on some irrelevant paperwork.

A.S.Chambers

The small, moustachioed man in the long, dark green jacket emblazoned with a golden letter M on the breast pocket nodded vigorously, seemingly ignorant of the policeman's discomfort. "Yes, yes. It was right in here."

Hallei-bloody-lujah! The cop rubbed at the nape of his neck with his free hand. Oh yes, last night had been a rough one, alright. That guy in forensics, the one who kept mixing up blood samples, had *finally* been let go. A group of them had headed out on the town to celebrate. It had started as pints, then shorts, then shots then… Well, he didn't quite remember. After two in the morning, it had become a total blur. All he knew for sure was that he'd woken up on someone's couch with a mouth that tasted like it had been playing sucky-sucky on the toes of a whore with a severe dose of athlete's foot.

He made the mistake of glancing down into the swirling brown liquid and his guts lurched.

Yeah, spending an hour wandering aimlessly around a chocolate factory was the last thing he needed today, but he was the one who'd got the call, so he was the one who had been told to get his shit together and play nice with the town's largest employer.

The McGilligan's brand was a powerhouse in the world of confectionery. Enticingly sweet goods left the twenty-acre site on the edge of town and were shipped all around the globe. Customers ranged in social status from the plebs in the street to kings and queens in their palaces. It was a well-known fact that should you have screwed up, then an emerald box embossed with a gold letter M was the ideal symbol of penitence. He himself had purchased numerous boxes over his long, chequered career, albeit from their cheaper ranges, after numerous screw-ups. The brand had hit the international diplomatic stage recently as the framed press cutting in the lobby had testified. There, as the world's politicians had sat down to thrash out the Damascus Accord, a large box of McGilligan's *Exultante* had been seated in the middle of the negotiation table, a suitable gift for all the international delegates from the summit's host.

So, as the taxi had driven his hung-over arse to the factory, the detective had told himself that he had been honoured by his superior in being given this particular, high-profile case. Now, however, after sixty minutes of tedium and the pervasive sickly odour of bubbling sugar and chocolate, he was having second thoughts.

An hour in and he hadn't even been told what had been nicked!

Time to put that right.

"So, can you please describe the thing that was stolen?" He wiped small pearls of sweat from his slick forehead before holding his pen expectantly over his pad.

The little man twitched and glanced down into the vat below them. "Well, isn't it obvious?"

The detective shook his head, immediately regretting the sudden movement. His stomach rolled over and he stifled a nauseating belch with the back of his hand. "Excuse me," he muttered.

His guide just peered at him oddly before replying: "Bubbles. Last night someone crept in under the cover of dark and stole a batch of bubbles!"

Yep, his sergeant had definitely done the dirty on him. "Bubbles? As in pockets of air?"

His guide nodded vigorously, his little moustache twitching from side to side. "Exactly. Just like the ones that appear to be bubbling around inside your stomach this morning," he smiled sheepishly. "A heavy night was it? Lots of fizzy beer?"

The cop grunted in annoyance, ignoring the intrusion into his personal life. He dragged the conversation back to the matter of the theft. "So, what? A gas? Some sort of cylinder, perhaps, that contains the substance you pump into your mix to aerate it?"

"No. No. Like I said, bubbles. Someone came in last night and purloined a batch of bubbles."

Perhaps he was still snoring his head off in a drunken stupor as he slept on a random stranger's couch? That would explain it. There was no way on God's green earth that he could be having this conversation. It was like that time he'd been arguing with a guy in the bar who was adamant that he'd been a member of a self-help cult led by an enigmatically charismatic leader. At first, the detective had dismissed the craziness as the rambling of a delusional drunk, but the guy had insisted that it had been true. He'd even told the cop the name of the group: Credete. So he'd gone as far as looking it up on his phone and received no hits. Big surprise. Just another nutter wandering the streets, then.

"That's because everything has changed," the drunk had insisted. "It's all changed: my home, my job, my entire life. It's all gone."

He had finally just patted the rummy on the back, left him a fiver for a drink in which to drown his delusion and walked out of the bar.

He couldn't do that here, not to a representative of the town's largest employer. The sergeant would staple his arse to the desk when he got back to the station.

Running his fingers through his less-than-immaculate hair, he dragged a tool out of the police kit bag that he was unaccustomed to utilising: diplomacy. "So, you have to understand that I'm not familiar with your production process. I'm just a simple layman and I don't know how this whole," he twirled his fingers around at the vat, "*thing* works. Could you please bear with me as you bring me up to speed?"

The little man shrugged. "There's not much to explain," he whined. "It's as I said. Someone came in and took a portion of our bubbles." He walked over to the handrail and pointed down into the vat of swirling chocolate below them. "Here, see for yourself."

The detective cautiously joined the company's representative at the handrail of the catwalk, placed a steadying hand on the refreshingly cold metal and, ignoring the swaying sensation in his stomach, peered over into the brown abyss.

"Do you see?"

Indeed he did. But how the hell was this possible? Down beneath the two of them, the voluminous brown mixture was being rotated by two large paddles that were controlled by an overhanging metal arm. As the paddles dragged their way through the thick chocolate, the sweet-smelling mixture lazily bubbled and popped.

Well, apart from in a metre square just below the catwalk.

There below them, apparently defying the laws of physics, was a perfect square of tranquillity. All around it the chocolate mixture merrily bubbled away. Here was what looked to the cop something akin to a set slab of brown cement. Yet, it couldn't be so as the paddles easily passed through on their revolving journey. Yet, each time they did, that square patch resolved to stay motionless and un-fluid, just closing up behind the paddle, taking on none of the bubbles in the surrounding mass of brown.

"That's not possible," he finally said.

"Well, obviously it is, because we're looking down at it," the smaller man protested.

"How the hell does someone just remove bubbles from something?"

The small man shrugged. "They used a box on a string? Lowered it down and scooped them up? A square one would leave the impression that we can see."

The cop turned to face his guide. "But, that's not possible. You can't just take bubbles from a liquid. They're… I don't know… a part of the liquid where the liquid isn't… I… I can't explain it."

"The bubbles are the most important part of our chocolate," the little man explained. "They are what gives our exquisite product its texture, its lightness. If you bite into a piece of McGilligan's confectionery it is like devouring a cloud. We are very proud of our process and that's why we strive to keep it secret. If anyone should manage to work out how we create the bubbles, then they could copy us and the market would collapse. It would be a financial disaster."

The cop waved his hand in protest. "I understand the need for professional secrecy, I do. But… bubbles. You can't take bubbles away from something. Well, not as a separate entity, that is. And, what's going on down there… No, it defies belief."

The small man's moustache twitched from side to side as he seemed to consider something. Finally, he asked, "Can I trust you?"

"Sure," the cop replied. Internally he just wanted to go home and escape this madness. Right now he would have said the sky was pink if it meant he could go home and have a lie down. "I'm a policeman. Of course you can trust me."

The company's representative nodded nervously and beckoned the detective to follow him along the catwalk. They reached a red door on a small platform overlooking the vats below. Next to it, a twisted mass of coloured tubes ran out along the metal arms to which the rotating paddles were attached.

"This," explained the man in a near whisper, "is where we make the bubbles."

The cop shrugged and gestured for him to lead on.

The small man led them into a tech-laden anteroom about the size of the detective's kitchen. The coloured tubes snaked their way around the walls and up to the ceiling. They terminated on the opposite wall above a plain alcove. The guide gestured for the cop to inspect the recess. "This is where the bubbles are made," he explained. "Right here is where the gaseous beauty is created that makes our chocolate *par excellence*."

The detective peered into the alcove. It ran from floor to ceiling. At the top, a large aperture seemed to lead up to what he guessed were the tubes that collected the bubbles. Around the side of the walls were what appeared to be small spray heads similar to those you found on sprinkler systems in offices and the like. "So, you insert a cylinder of gas in here?"

"Not exactly."

The cop felt a rough shove in the base of his back and he stumbled into the alcove. Swearing, he turned to be confronted with a clear glass panel shooting up in front of him. He banged frantically on the solid glass as the company man proceeded to fiddle with controls on a discreet panel. A hissing noise filled the cop's ears, deafening in the enclosed space and a sour stench enveloped him as a clear liquid spurted out of the jets. He hammered again on the glass but the crazy guy outside just ignored him.

Then there was agony.

He'd never felt anything like it before. As the liquid coated his skin he felt a searing sensation overwhelming him. He juddered and writhed as he felt the substance digging its way inside of him, through his veins and arteries, burrowing deeper and deeper inside, down towards his stomach. A giant spasm overcame him and his back whacked against the wall of the alcove as he felt the most excruciating pain in his guts that he had ever known. It was as if someone was lowering him down onto the blades of a gigantic blender. He started to scream as he watched his shirt rip open, his skin expanding through the torn material. The skin was rolling, undulating in a cruel mimicry of pregnancy. Something was there, waiting to be born, to erupt into this world. The detective's eyes were wide as he continued to scream, but now no sound would come. Instead, there was a hissing of gas building in his throat. All he could do was open his mouth as the hiss quickly became a roar and he watched as red bubbles began to roll out from over his speechless tongue.

But the gas wasn't just coming from his mouth.

He stared in horrified stupefaction as the skin on the back of his hands began to evaporate. Small bubbles began to rise up between the black hairs and drifted up to the tubes above. The first ones were clear but they were soon followed by red companions.

The cop's legs turned to jelly and he slumped against the wall, unable to fall completely to the floor due to the cramped space. At first, all he could do was watch as his body began to dissolve into a light gas, but then all he could do was scream silently as he was transformed into bubbles, until finally all he could do was die.

After five minutes, the short man with the moustache stepped away from the console. Without so much as a glance at the bubble chamber, he exited the anteroom and walked carefully along the catwalk. Peering down into the chocolate below, he studied the plain square fearfully.

Eventually, after what seemed like a lifetime, bubbles started to form around the regular edges, easing their way into the centre of the erroneous shape until finally the chocolate was covered once more with a mass of small bubbles that would bring delight to discerning palates around the world.

The small man nodded to himself and turned to head out of the room, cheerfully whistling to himself.

Lifting The Veil

Aaron stared down into the void.

The void stared back up at him. In fact, it clapped its hands together before holding them out and crying, "Come on in and let me give you a great big hug!"

A great big hug... What he would give for one of those right about now. But it wasn't going to happen, was it? Certainly not from Joyce, his foster mother of fifteen years. No, she thought he was a complete waste of space. All she ever banged on about were his poor grades and lack of progress.

"Why do you constantly have to let me down, Aaron?

"Why don't you pay more attention at school, Aaron?

"Why did you set fire to the maths teacher's jacket, Aaron?"

Okay, to be fair, she probably had a bit of a right to be pissed at him for that last one, but the lesson had just been so dull. Sourface Solomon always had it in for him. He'd deserved it. And it wasn't like Aaron could have stopped himself. The guy had been bending over and the back of that grey tweed jacket had just been calling to him, like the void was right now.

"Come to me!" it had cried out. "Set me on fire!"

So, he had. He'd just whipped out the little Bic he carried everywhere, the one with the woman and the disappearing dress he'd nicked in Normandy last summer, and he'd simply set fire to the hem of Sourpuss' jacket.

The rest of the class had thought it was hilarious!

Like all the other random stuff he did: running down the corridor the wrong way whilst quacking like a duck; flicking that weird pink pudding up in the air that they served at dinner and catching it in his mouth; drawing a large dick on the tech teacher's whiteboard before they began the lesson.

Aaron thought of his pranks as the stuff of legend. Why couldn't his mum? He was just having some fun.

It took his mind off the gut-wrenching nightmares.

Aaron's stomach lurched and he blocked the images from his mind as his feet shuffled closer to the edge of the parapet of the Lune Aqueduct.

But, it wasn't just his mum, was it?

There was Vikki, too.

Oh god, there was Vikki!

Shuffle, shuffle...

As he stared down into the dark waters on the warm April night, Aaron tried to blot out the girl's face, but the look she had given him refused to vanish. It had been one of first shock then derision. She had turned to her mates and just guffawed with laughter before they'd walked down the corridor, sniggering to each other. He had been left standing with everyone else just staring at him, his cheeks reddening.

The thing was, he had been so sure. He had been

convinced that she'd go with him to the *Kidsweek* party on Saturday. She'd been giving him the eye all week. He was sure of it. She'd looked at him in Physics, smiled at him in English and walked really close to him in French. Surely that all meant that she'd wanted to be his date?

So, he'd readied himself. He'd brushed his hair, checked his teeth and doused himself in an extra coating of Lynx before approaching her on the way to Maths, confident that he would receive a positive answer.

But, no. She'd laughed at him.

Like he was a joke. Just one, big joke.

Well, the joke was on her. Yes, it was. She wouldn't be laughing when they pulled his corpse out of the Lune, would she? She wouldn't be sniggering to her mates at the back of the crematorium when those curtains slid shut.

No, there would be tears. Lots of tears. Vikki's, his foster mum's and anyone else who secretly thought he was an idiot.

"I can't wait to see their faces," Aaron spat as he rubbed tears away from his cheek with the heel of his hand.

"Personally, I think your logic is flawed," came a voice from behind him that sounded like a thousand boulders rolling down a mountain.

The teenage boy turned, startled, to see who had spoken and gasped as his eyes were confronted with a giant stone monster. Instinctively, he took a panicked step backwards.

The night air grabbed his foot and he began to fall.

It was like one of those moments when someone's nodding off to sleep and they feel like they're falling down a great chasm or out of a plane. For a completely inexplicable reason they are no longer in bed but are somewhere at a great height and the ground beneath their feet has vanished, causing them to be plummeting down, down, down. The wind rushes up, buffeting their clothes and flowing through their hair. As he fell backwards, down towards the crashing waters of the River Lune, Aaron remembered a biology lesson when they had learnt about this phenomenon: a hypnic jerk. For whatever reason, the brain got confused as the body drifted off to sleep and translated the sensation of the muscles relaxing as the individual falling. Then, after every great fall, came a juddering impact caused by the brain snapping the body out of the confusing freefall.

He had listened fascinated for once. He was familiar with this sensation. It came almost every night now. He'd be drifting off to sleep and would feel his heavy feet crash to the floor with a sickening thud, jarring his entire body.

At least *this* fall would be the end of all that and the gruesome horrors that always followed.

Aaron closed his eyes and waited for the non-dream-state smashing of his body into the waters and rocks below.

However, this particular night, the jerk came in a most unexpected manner.

He screamed out as his body cracked to a sudden halt a few metres above the rushing current. Opening his eyes, he lifted them from the swirling waters below and up towards a large stone hand that was wrapped around his ankle. Attached to the hand was a giant stone arm that belonged to the creature that had startled him on the aqueduct. Behind the monster beat two large stone wings.

73

And, was that a bowler hat duct-taped to its head?

Aaron felt himself begin to slowly rise back up into the night air and presently, the creature lay him gently on the cycle path that crossed the aqueduct. The teenage boy back-crawled away from his winged saviour and pressed himself up against the balustraded parapet. He wanted to say something, but no words would come. There, hunkering down in front of him, peering with curiosity was something that shouldn't exist. It was a moving statue, easily three times his size, with a huge pair of wings folded neatly behind its back.

And, yes it had a bowler hat duct taped to its head.

"In answer to the question that you cannot bring yourself to ask," rumbled the sound of a cliff cascading into an ocean, "my name is Spud and please accept my profoundest apologies for startling you like that."

All Aaron could do was open and shut his mouth repeatedly.

"You appear to be having some trouble processing the actuality of my existence," rumbled the deep, gravelly voice. "I find this most peculiar considering recent events?"

"*Ree*..." Once Aaron had rediscovered the ability of speech, the first syllable he tried came out as a high-pitched squeak. He coughed, cleared his throat and tried again. "Recent events?"

The stone creature that called itself Spud nodded once and pointed to a mobile phone that it had duct taped to its wrist in a similar fashion that the hat was fastened to its head. "The vampire immolating itself on Sunday. I am sure you witnessed that on your own little device. The footage *did* go viral after all."

The boy frowned as his mind raced to work out

what the creature was talking about. "Oh…" he eventually said. "Yeah. I saw that. My mum said it was a practical stunt. Isn't everything these days? Everyone wants to get famous."

The animated statue grunted. "And that is what you believe?"

"Well, it has to be."

"And why is that?"

"Because… because things like that… don't…" Aaron heard his words get gradually quieter as uncertainty muffled them, "exist…"

Spud raised a stone eyebrow.

Aaron swallowed. "It was real, wasn't it?"

The statue ran a taloned finger across its chin. A noise like two boulders rubbing against each other resonated in the night air. "There is a veil that covers your reality," Spud said, his grey eyes fixed on the teenager. "Your species tell yourself that it's not there, yet you gratefully pull it down over yourselves and look pointedly away from the shadows that move on the other side of the thin material. Sometimes, however, the creatures on the other side come to peer at you as you go about your lives under the false security that you believe the veil provides you. Mostly they stand on the other side of the thin material and watch you with a mixture of curiosity and amusement, bemused at how you refuse to accept that there are creatures lurking in the shadows around you. They shake their heads and walk away despairing at how over the course of so many millennia, you have relegated their kind to the stuff of legend and fairy tale, or even an *internet prank*.

"However, every now and then, one of their kind will lift the edge of the veil and will walk unimpeded into your

75

world. And, when they are there, carnage will ensue, just as it did down on the quayside back at the end of January."

Aaron frowned. "I don't…"

"Remember?" asked the creature. "Of course you don't. The creatures that ran rampant in this beautiful city were, to your kind, just the things of old legends or stories concerning beasts that try to lure a young girl in a red cape away from the path before devouring her granny."

Realisation dawned on the teenage boy. "You… you're talking about werewolves?"

Spud nodded.

"There was the stuff on the news," Aaron continued. "People dressing up as wolves or something. Was that connected?"

The creature's shoulders seemed to rise and fall as if it were sighing deeply. "Someone pushed the creatures back out from under the veil. They will never return."

"This…" Aaron hesitated to say the word, "…vampire. Is he one who has crawled under the veil?"

Spud shook his head. "No. Poor Marcus was the one who was destined to set fire to it and remove it permanently."

"So, this girl, Vikki, you have romantic feelings for her?"

Just twenty minutes previously, Aaron had been standing on top of a bridge, contemplating jumping into the waters below and ending his miserable life. Now, not only did he know that the monsters from under the bed were real, but he had just ridden on the back of one of them across to the other side of town. Climbing down off Spud's wide shoulders, he settled his feet on the firm ground of Vikki's back garden. "She's hot," he said. "Plus, I thought she liked me."

The statue's finger grated against his cheek. "By *hot,* am I to understand that she is physically attractive rather than likely to combust?"

Aaron grinned. "Yep. I can't get her out of my head. It's like I'm burning up."

"Hmmm… Emotions. I see. Not something that I am used to." Spud tapped his chest. "No organs within me that could produce the correct brain chemicals. Come to think of it, no brain either."

"So, how do you, you know, do what you do?"

Spud stretched his wings out behind him before settling them into a relaxed position. "Move? Oh, that's quite simple. Magic. The man who created me was talented in more arts than just exquisite carving of finely chiselled abs." One of the grotesque's eyelids slowly lowered then rose again in an approximation of a wink. "So, the young girl of your dreams resides here, then?"

Aaron blanched at the mention of the word *dreams*. Again he felt the sensation of his feet crashing heavily to the ground beneath him. He saw his hand reach out…

The teenager shook his head. "Yeah. Sure. Girl of my dreams. I can't get her out of my head. She's all I think about."

Spud slowly cocked his head to one side and studied the boy.

"What?"

"I think you dream about more than just this girl."

"Yeah, well, what of it?"

The grotesque turned his head towards the house, "Just an observation. Tell me. If this girl was to agree to a romantic proposition from you, what then?"

"I just wanted her to go to the *Kidsweek* disco with me at the weekend," Aaron shrugged. "That's all."

"You have no further intentions?"

"Ah, gross, man. Come on!"

"In my observations, many humans of your age seem to consider practising for the reproduction of their species to be a very dominant activity."

"Jesus, you sound like my Biology teacher..."

"But, it is true. Would you want this girl to be your lifelong mate?"

"How the hell would I know? I've not even got to cop a feel at a sodding disco!"

"But you must know more about her than just the feeling that she is *hot*, surely? You must know what her interests are, how she spends her spare time and what she considers to be important issues. Surely these are important factors for choosing a mate?"

"I'm sixteen. Those sorts of things don't really factor into my thoughts that much."

Spud held the teenage boy in an unmoving stare. "Perhaps they should? Over the centuries, society has performed a very curious thing to humans of your age."

"Oh? What's that, then?"

"More and more, it has expected you to act mature whilst staying younger longer. When I was created, a boy of thirteen was more or less an adult. He was given either a hoe for the field or a pike for the battleground and was told, "Don't take your eye out with the pointy end. Now, though... Now, you are not considered an adult until you are much older. Sixteen, eighteen, twenty-one, twenty-five... These ages are all arbitrary, especially when, even though you are still seen as children, you are expected to act as if you have twenty years more experience in your life. It is no wonder you make so many mistakes. Society does not know what to do with you. It wants to protect you but also expects you to learn without enduring any mishaps."

"Mishaps," Aaron grunted. "I've had plenty of those. Ask my mother."

"I have observed that a good parent wants what's best for their child. You talk as if she is criticising you. Perhaps she is just worried?"

"Perhaps," the boy shrugged. "I don't know…" He turned to the grotesque. "So, why are we here exactly?"

"We are here so that you can make an informed decision," rumbled the voice that was akin to a mountain collapsing in upon itself. "You have feelings for this girl, Vikki, yet you do not really know her."

"So, what? You're suggesting I just knock on her door and ask for a chat?"

The grotesque inclined his head. "No. You would either be ridiculed again or she would present a face that was false for the sake of appearances. I suggest that you get to know the *real* Vikki." With that, he scooped Aaron up in one arm and began to climb up the wall of the suburban house.

Aaron was amazed at how silently the animated statue was able to move. As its feet and free hand moved in perfect harmony, there wasn't even the slightest suggestion that a gargantuan winged beast was carrying a teenage boy up the side of a house. Vikki's family wouldn't have a clue inside.

Shortly, they were perched beside an open window. Carefully, Aaron peered inside before snatching his head back. "This is the right one. She's in there."

"As I knew she would be."

"How?"

"I have very acute hearing. I could hear her chattering from down below."

Aaron nodded. Vikki was talking to someone on her mobile. He frowned. "What if someone sees us?"

Spud raised an eyebrow. "The stone grotesque holding a teenage boy onto the side of a house?"

"Yeah. That's the one. Won't it look odd?"

"Odder than werewolves or a combusting vampire?"

"Point taken." Aaron adjusted himself in Spud's arm and drew as close as he could to the open window without being seen. His new friend had a point. At school, he'd always admired Vikki from afar, so to speak. He'd never had an actual conversation with her. This was due partly to his own insecurity but also to the fact that she was normally part of her little gaggle of friends. They were like an impenetrable wall, unable to be breached by random intruders. To be honest, the only time he had ever heard her speak was when she was forced to answer questions in class, which she normally did with sullen acceptance and an eye roll.

After just five minutes, he said to his companion. "Can you take me home please?"

The grotesque nodded, flapped its wings and they soared up into the night sky. As Lancaster spread out beneath them, the flying statue waited patiently for the boy to speak.

"She's not what I expected."

The grotesque concentrated on flying unobserved, allowing Aaron time to gather his thoughts.

"I always thought she'd be bright, you know? Intelligent? I mean, she *looks* it, so she should act it. Does that make sense?"

Spud replied with a silent nod.

"But... but what they were talking about..." Aaron shook his head. "It was just mean. Mate, they were slagging off *one of their friends*! That's not on. Not on. This is one of the girls who's always hanging with her — someone she sees every day and is as nice as pie to. The things they were calling her back there..." He drifted away, lost in thought as Spud circled above the teenager's house.

"I have observed," rumbled the grotesque, "in my long existence, that most people are not what they seem. They have a public face and a private one, one that they keep to themselves."

Aaron nodded. "Yeah, I bet when she got off the phone she'll have rung someone else and started slagging off the girl she'd just been talking to. That sucks. People should just be what they are. Life would be a lot easier if that were the case." He shuddered.

"Are you okay, Aaron?"

The teenager swallowed. "Yeah." He flexed his fingers back and forth. "I'm good. I think you just lifted my veil for me."

The grotesque nodded and landed gently in the garden behind Aaron's house. "I hope that's a good thing. It is right that we should be true to who we are."

"Sure thing." The teenager stepped down from the grotesque's arms and rolled his neck. His head felt incredibly heavy. "Hey. Thanks for tonight."

"It was nothing," came the sound of pyroclastic flow descending upon a barren valley.

"No, man. It was a big deal." The boy stepped forward and wrapped his arms around the statue. After a brief hug, he drew back and headed towards his house. "See you around, big guy."

For a moment, the statue with a bowler hat taped to its head watched the boy walk away before it flapped its stone wings and soared up into the night sky.

Be myself: Aaron thought to himself as he locked the back door. *That's what I need to do. Just be myself.* He cricked his neck around once again and felt the tension he had been carrying for many months now simply slip away. Yeah. He could be himself. He could do that.

"Where the hell have you been?" His foster mother was standing blocking the door from the kitchen to the hallway. Her arms were crossed accusingly across her chest. "If you've been out shagging some girl…"

A smile touched the boy's lips. "No. Nothing like that."

"You been nicking stuff again? Is that it?"

"No. I've been taught how to see clearly. I've lifted the veil." He lifted his hand and studied the five fingers in front of him. Somewhere else, his foster mother, the woman who had taken him in as a baby, was ranting and raving about how he should be grateful for all she had done for him; about how she had provided food on the table and a roof over his head when no one had wanted him.

But he did not hear her.

All he could hear as he continued to study the fingers in front of him was the pounding of his heart.

Thud… thud…

But it wasn't a heart, was it? It was the same sound that he heard every night in his dreams.

Thud… thud…

Hear My Scare

The marching of heavy feet across a barren landscape. The marching of soldiers fulfilling the purpose for which they had been created.

The pointless voice was uttering banal words as Aaron watched his fingers fuse together into their true form. His smile spread wider than humanly possible and he reached out across the room with his long arm.

The woman's words drew to a shuddering halt as the lance rammed through her heart. Her eyes widened and blood pooled up from her open mouth, drooling down her chin.

The creature withdrew its arm and studied the contents of the human that remained on its grey-brown surface.

It nodded.

In its head, the construct saw an image of it marching with its kindred across a field a few miles from town. Before them was an old farmhouse with a ramshackle barn off to the side. The stench of prey reached the long black tongue that slathered out of its deformed mouth. It closed its eyes and acknowledged the order before turning and stalking out of the dead human's house.

Appeasing The Gods

Howard Swales swore under his breath as he lugged the Vent-A-Matic 2000 up yet another bland suburban driveway. This particular gravel-covered entrance to a middle-class kingdom on the edge of town was flanked by diminutive figurines of gaudily painted gnomes standing sentinel, armed with their tiny array of gardening paraphernalia and fishing tackle. He cursed once again as the wheels on the wretched vacuum cleaner stuck in the small stones of the drive. He jerked it free and stumbled, almost taking out a small guard. He was sure that the damn appliance was beginning to weigh more than a baby elephant. He'd taken Janet to see a group of elephants the last time the circus had been in town. All the darned animals had done was suck stuff up with their ridiculous noses before shitting it out the other end.

Rather like the stupid vacuum cleaners he sold.

In one end, out the other. Pointless pieces of foreign crap. Why did folks think they needed the latest gadget these days anyway? It hadn't been like that when he'd been a kid. You just got down on your knees with a good old dustpan and brush then swept the stuff up that you'd spilt. Five seconds; job done. Now you had to drag the vacuum cleaner out of the closet, unravel the flex, move the sofa to plug it in, realise you hadn't emptied the darned bag the last time you'd used it, empty the bag, re-place the bag, suck the crud up whilst being deafened by a cacophony of noise louder than a pachyderm on heat, then finally tidy all the clutter away.

Absolute waste of time and money if you asked him.

Not that he could tell his potential customers that, of course. No, sir! He needed those sales; needed the good hard cash.

Or rather, Eddie the Mallet needed the readies. Howard had made quite a number of unfortunate choices on the horses over the last few months and now it was time to pay up. Pay up or remember how Eddie got his name...

Howard shuddered at that thought as he knocked brightly on the latest door, a glossy red affair that was edged with all manner of hand-painted yellow flowers and swirling patterns. *Someone likes their arts and crafts, then*: the salesman thought to himself.

He was just about to knock for the second time when there was the rattling of a key in the lock. The brightly-coloured door swung inwards and Howard was greeted by the smiling face of a white-haired woman who looked like she had left eighty in the dust years ago. "Hello, young man?" Her voice was creaky with age, but still light in timbre. Her arthritic fingers shook slightly as they held the edge of the front door. "How can I help you?"

Howard launched into his set spiel about how he was in the neighbourhood with the world's newest, greatest invention, *blah blah blah*... As the words fell from his tongue, he realised that this was going to be just another waste of time and another step nearer to getting up close and personal with his loan shark's favourite toy. There was no way that this old crone was going to want to fork out for a modern appliance. Hell, she probably still swept around the house every morning with the same dustpan and brush she'd used for the last sixty years, ferreting around for dust bunnies as they skittered along the skirting board of her *parlour*.

Needless to say, he was stunned when he reached the end of his doorstep pitch and she called into the house, "Arthur, make some iced tea! We've got company."

The insides of the house proved to be somewhat of a revelation to Howard Swales. There was no dingy *parlour,* decked out with an overstuffed couch that was bedecked with an ancient crocheted throw or a faux fur rug in front of an old coal fire. Instead, the front room was decidedly spacious, its modern decor and furniture seemingly at odds with its octogenarian occupants. A new-looking, tastefully fashionable suite swept around the corner of the room, the focal point of which was a decidedly modern oil painting on the main wall. It was upon the long couch that the elderly couple sat expectantly as the salesman prepped his Vent-A-Matic 2000 for its demonstration.

"That's a fine-looking bit of kit you've got there, sonny," commented the husband. "It sure looks like a modern wonder with all those dials and tubes and such."

"Indeed it is, sir," Howard beamed. This was going to be a piece of cake! The couple were hanging off his every word. They'd already nodded appreciatively as he'd explained about the vacuum's ten-year warranty and its cutting-edge filtration system. "It's designed to be the only piece of domestic cleaning equipment that you'll ever need."

The elderly housewife clapped her gnarled hands together. "Well, isn't that just marvellous! Imagine all the time and effort it will save me."

It was impossible for Howard to hide his grin as he plugged the vacuum into a socket underneath the large oil painting. As he stood up, he came face to face with a riot of primary colours dashed with blobs of oranges and limes. His eyes were drawn deeper into racing brush strokes and scooped ridges of paint. "I have to say, I wouldn't have pegged you as modern art fanatics."

The old man chuckled as he poured a cup of iced tea for their guest. "Well, looks can be deceptive, can't they? We feel it brightens the room and provides a nice conversation piece."

Howard nodded. "You can say that again."

"Plus, it's worth just shy of a million. Sugar?"

For a moment, Howard found it impossible to co-ordinate his voice box, his teeth and his tongue. *Just shy of a million? Hanging on the wall of some old dears' living room?* He swallowed, his gaze still fixed on the crazed creation of some acid-tripping artist. Eventually, he managed, "How did you come by it?"

"Well, that's a funny story, really," the old woman began. "We were out for a good old jolly in the country a few weeks back when we saw that someone was having a yard sale. I can't remember the finer points exactly; someone had died, I think, and the kids were getting rid of all the clutter as they do these days. Anyway, the picture was propped up against the wall of the house and we went and had a look at it. They practically begged us to take it. Pleaded, they did. We guessed that it wasn't really

87

to their taste. So, we decided that we might as well. When we got it home, we thought we might as well get it valued. Imagine our surprise when it turned out to be by some famous chap that neither of us had ever heard of."

"Fancy that…" Howard's voice was little more than a whisper as certain cogs and gears began to engage in his head. A dark machine was starting to rev itself up, spurting black smoke from its exhaust before commencing its trundling journey down a highway that could get Eddie the Mallet off his back for good. It involved an elderly couple, a fancy painting, a back door and a crowbar. He swallowed and ran a hand up and down his neck as the eddies of paint on the canvas appeared to reach out to him. "Fancy that…" he repeated. "What's it called?"

"Appeasing the Gods," the old guy explained. "Apparently it's a depiction of an individual's mind when they are faced with seemingly unsurmountable tasks that need to be undertaken to satisfy those who pull their strings, so to speak."

An image of Eddie the Mallet sitting behind his desk whilst cracking his knuckles drifted into Howard's head. "Ain't that the truth…" As the imagined agony of cracked bones brought a sweat to his forehead, he almost missed what the old timer said next.

"Yes, indeed. The thing is, the particular artist of this piece seemed to have somewhat of a more apocalyptic view of that matter."

The salesman frowned. "What do you mean?"

"It would seem that he believed in old vengeful deities from before time itself that could simply sweep us away if they weren't satisfied with our lot in life. This work of art was the last thing that he created. It was supposed to be part of his therapy as he spent time in an insane asylum."

"You said it was his last work… I'm guessing the therapy didn't work out all that good?"

The old man shook his head. "He was found dead at the foot of this, his final masterpiece. It seems that his heart gave out."

Howard continued to stare at the crazed frenzy of oils that swept around the canvas. Bright primary colours seemed to run side by side in whirling spirals before cris-scrossing and blending into a startling array of different shades and hues. Shapes and patterns lurked beneath numerous brush strokes: some abstract, some almost geometric. It was as if the canvas before him was the entire world — a mad world created by a crazed god imprisoned in a padded cell.

The salesman jumped slightly as he felt a tall glass being pushed into his hand and he was dragged back into the living room of two elderly art lovers. Looking down, he saw the tumbler of iced tea. A nice and normal reminder of the real world around him. Yes, a real world that consisted of a sociopathic loan shark who had a penchant for heavy hammers, a guy who had been unfortunate enough to get into debt with said money lender and a pair of old crusties who had happened upon a valuable piece of art. Lifting the glass, he drank slowly and a plan began to evolve in his head. He could come back tonight, when the old codgers were asleep. That would work. Yes, it would. It was a large house and they were probably hard of hearing. They wouldn't hear him breaking in, grabbing the picture and making a run for it. Eddie would be paid off by the end of the week and he'd have a considerable bundle of cash left over. No more selling useless vacuum cleaners.

The old guy was saying something else, but

Howard couldn't make out the words. The colours and shapes of the painting held him completely enrapt as he stared at the thing that would change his life around completely. With no Eddie on his case, he would be a free man. Hell, what would this old couple do with this painting anyway? It's not like they were going to sell it and use the money to go out and buy more iced tea.

He swallowed another sip of the drink.

A crescent of lime oil paint on the picture flicked from side to side.

What the hell?

The crescent stretched out as Howard stood and stared. The scythe-like shape lengthened and elongated, wet suckers bursting from its underside. A slash of orange in the middle of the picture split down the middle, exposing a black void in its midst. The orange snapped back and forth like a hungry beak and Howard could hear a harsh cawing noise emanating from the obsidian hole. He took a step back but the lime green tentacle whipped out and encircled his neck. He screamed and the glass tumbler fell to the floor as the limb dragged him forward to the hungry, gnashing mouth. The last thing he saw, before the painting devoured him, was the elderly couple sitting on their couch with benevolent smiles on their faces.

When Howard Swales, purveyor of cheap imported electronics and debtor to local loan shark Eddie the Mallet, awoke he found himself tied firmly to a hard wooden table. He yanked at his arms but they were fastened tight, as were his legs. He tried to lift his head but the world around him swam with bright, hazy colours. He closed his eyes and slowly reopened them when the nausea had passed.

Hear My Scare

He was in a dimly lit room that looked decidedly like a cellar. A cellar? What was a modern house in the suburbs doing with a cellar? The only illumination was from numerous pillar candles that were dotted around the low-ceilinged room. Black candles, he noted. On the ceiling above him were scrawled numerous, unintelligible scribblings. They appeared to have been painted on in red paint, but he had a sinking feeling that he might be mistaken about that.

There was the sound of whispering.

Howard cautiously craned his neck in the direction of the noise. There, to his horror were the elderly couple. They were stark naked! Hearing his movement, they stopped their low-volume conversation and walked over to the table. Howard tried his best to look anywhere apart from the numerous sagging appendages that swayed left and right as they bent over him. "What... what's going on?" he managed.

"I'm terribly sorry about the drink," the old man apologised. "We just find it the easiest way to immobilise people."

"Erm... okay. Apology accepted. Now, if you could please untie me?"

The octogenarians shook their heads in unison. "I'm afraid we can't do that," the woman sighed, "as much as we'd love to. You see, the painting wants you."

"Wants?"

"Yes, it hungers and it needs to be fed." She reached out to the top of the table upon which the would-be art thief was trussed and produced a long sharp kitchen knife. "Our existence depends on satisfying it. If it feels we are unworthy then it will discard us. All will become black."

Howard began to thrash wildly at his bonds. "Look. Please. Just let me go. I'll never come back. I won't tell anyone about this."

"But then the picture would still be hungry," the old man explained. "And we can't have that, can we?" He nodded to his wife and Howard clenched his eyes shut and screamed into the room as the blade plunged downwards.

There was no pain.

There was no oblivion.

There was no fiery pit.

There was silence.

Howard Swales, vacuum cleaner salesman and potential art thief, nervously cracked open his right eye. The knife hovered just above his sternum. The same shake that he had noticed in the old dear's hand as she had opened the door now caused the knife to quiver threateningly above his chest.

"Oh, Arthur!" she wailed. "I can't do this. It just isn't right!"

The old boy nodded, slipped his wrinkled hands around the knife and prised it from her gnarled fingers. "I know, Eunice. I know." He sighed, bent over and undid the straps that held their potential sacrifice bound to the table. Then, turning to his wife, he wrapped her in his arms and cradled her as she sobbed into his neck.

As touching as the scene may have been, Howard had no desire for the crazy couple to have a change of heart. As soon as his limbs were free, he jumped down from the table and sped up the stairs of the cellar. Dashing through the house, he made a point of not going back into the living room to collect the Vent-A-Matic 2000. No way was he going to go anywhere near that terrifying

92

painting again. Let the old couple keep the wretched machine. He was done with the sales business.

As he ran out of the front door and hurried up the road to his awaiting car, he decided that there were indeed some things more terrifying in life than a loan shark with a mallet.

Rain hammered against the window. Luke Davies sat back in the office chair he'd bought online for far more than it was actually worth and stared at the screen of the computer on his desk.

He groaned and ran a tired hand over his face.

He hated deadlines. Whenever they loomed, he seemed to go into free fall. As a result, he ended up writing any old crap. His agent had rung yesterday morning, saying that a manuscript for the next book was expected to be in the editor's inbox by Wednesday.

Davies looked up at the fantasy art calendar pinned to his wall. That was in two days' time and he was still missing one more short for the anthology.

And what had he produced? A hatchet job on something he'd first concocted when he'd been at university! He reread the story and winced at every well-trodden cliche and trope: guy in debt, mysterious painting, an elderly couple with a gnome fixation. For crying out loud, even the main character had realised that their house shouldn't have a cellar! Couldn't he have used a summerhouse or something?

And, why the hell had the damned salesman been spared? He was an utter toad who would happily have robbed a pair of pensioners blind to save his own neck. Davies shook his head. The old couple should have killed him on the sacrificial table rather than letting him get away.

He huffed in annoyance and closed the document.

No, it wouldn't do at all. He'd have to come up with something else with which to satisfy his editor.

Using his mouse, he dragged the story and the world within it to his recycle bin.

Metamorphosis

Keith Templeton always enjoyed his walk home. In fact, he would go so far as to say it was the best part of the day. Not that he really had any *bad* parts to his day; it was just that this was the best of a wonderful bunch of events in a life that he considered idyllic.

He paused under one of the tall beech trees lining the park that he passed twice a day. Smiling up at the lush green leaves of late summer, he reckoned that he could just make out a slight discolouration to the leaves. Nodding to himself, he recalled the chilly temperatures last night. Yep, autumn was on its way and the coming darker weather would cause the chlorophyll levels to drop. The dense, bright green canopy of the trees that had accompanied him on his daily journeys to and from work over the past months would quickly depart. In its place would remain the stark, leafless sentinels awaiting the return of next year's spring.

Keith suddenly noticed a clump of leaves twitch and a beaming grin formed on his face as a bundle of grey fur bounced into view.

"Well, hello, little chap," he called up to the squirrel.

"How are you this evening?" He felt a cracking sensation under the sole of his sensible, leather-soled Oxford and looked down to see cast-off beech nut casings. "Ah, you can feel it too, can you? You're stocking up for winter. Good for you!"

The squirrel momentarily peered down at the figure below before scampering back into the safety of the tree's foliage.

Keith nodded to himself. "Sensible little chap. Pays to be prepared. You never know what's around the corner. Get stocked up for you and yours." A warm image came to mind of the squirrel hunkering down in its drey with its mate and child. Keith glanced down at the glowing display of his digital watch and whistled. He'd better get a move on and hurry home to his own little family unit. It wouldn't be fair to keep Maureen waiting. She'd have made one of her gorgeous casseroles tonight and he wouldn't want it to spoil. She always put so much effort into getting the level of savoury and spice just right. Casserole night was one of the highlights of Keith's week. It was wonderful to be able to sit around the dining table and eat as a family, the three of them. So many folks just didn't make time for that chance to bond, to swap the stories of the day with one another. Sure, he was the one who did most of the talking, Maureen had never been the chatty type and their son was going through his awkward teenage phase right now, but Keith prided himself on being the glue that bonded them together.

Sure, Keith worried about his son every now and then, but that was perfectly natural, wasn't it? As he continued his walk home, he considered that perhaps the media should put a bit more thought and consideration into some of the news stories they ran. All these tales of dysfunctional families couldn't really do people any good, could they? These dark tales of family neuroses just made folks paranoid and got them looking for problems that weren't actually there. Consequently, those problems were manufactured by engendering a feeling of unsettlement when there hadn't actually been any before. No, his lad was okay. He was just a boy in his mid-teens, going through the same changes that his father had at that age. He would just be wondering about his place in the world, feeling the hormones starting to kick in and beginning to feel the call of nature for him to spread his wings and fly.

Keith knew that he would have been the same. It was perfectly natural. He was sure that he had stomped off to his room in sullen silence on more than one occasion. He thought back thirty-odd years and recalled the same sort of thing.

At least, he tried to.

As hard as he pushed at the distant memories of puberty, there was nothing. No awkward silences, no despairing at embarrassing parents, no slamming of doors at the unfairness of everything. Keith shrugged and smiled. Ah well, perhaps it had been easier back then. These days, kids were constantly bombarded from every angle with television, the internet and all that sort of stuff. It was no wonder they retreated into themselves as they did. As long as they knew you loved them, they would be all right in the end.

And Keith made sure that his son knew that every single morning. He made it part of his daily ritual to tousle the lad's mop of dark hair and say, "Morning, Champ," before heading off to work. It was these little daily rituals that made children feel safe and grounded. Things out of the ordinary just upset them, distressed them.

Let's face it: he thought to himself. *That never changes, no matter how old you are.*

Even as adults, people didn't like being out of their comfort zone. Especially in the workplace. Crikey! There had been that incident at work, just today, hadn't there? They'd all been sat in the staffroom at lunchtime, working their way through their own individual pack-ups. Brian had his usual tuna mayo on white, Ivan his roast beef leftovers with mustard on granary and Susan her salmon and cucumber. He had been tucking into his daily repast of red Leicester and Branston. They had been sitting in companionable silence, just eating their sandwiches when a news flash came on the radio. One minute, they had been listening to that smooth jazz channel that was popular right now — it was the perfect background music for the downtime they shared during the busy work day. The next, a reporter was reading out a statement that the government of Israel had just made, saying that they would not stand for the recent escalation of attacks in Jerusalem. The reporter had read in a dispassionate, monotone voice that the government of Israel would meet such deplorable acts of terrorism with the full might of its well-trained, incredibly well-funded army. Blood would be shed as in battles of old until the blight was eradicated from the nation.

Well, it had certainly put everyone off their sandwiches, that was for sure.

They had all sat there for a while, staring in disbelief at the radio. None of them had been able to comprehend why the station had felt the need to share such disturbing news during the middle of the day. "They could have waited until teatime," Ivan grumbled, wrapping his roast beef and mustard back into its foil. "Why, on earth, did they have to make such a big thing about it right now? At lunchtime!"

Susan shook her head. "Well, this just takes me back to when I was young. There were bombs going off all over the place and it wasn't safe to travel on planes."

"I remember that." Ivan had stashed his discarded packed lunch next to his sales spreadsheets that resided in his leather satchel and was sitting forward on his chair. "My parents were going hairless. We had this holiday booked for Calais one summer and my mother didn't want to go in case we got blown up. My dad tried to reassure her that a cross-channel ferry to Normandy was hardly the same as flying out to Beirut, but she was having none of it." He sighed. "That year was the first of many deadly dull trips to Blackpool."

"Do you think it'll come to anything?"

All eyes turned to face Brian. The grey accounts manager was normally taciturn on all matters except for invoicing and debt collection.

"I mean. Could we get dragged into this? My father was out there years ago. He said it was an awful affair. First, we were fighting one lot, then we were helping them... A right ruddy mess, he used to call it."

Keith swallowed his piece of cheese and pickle sandwich. "It's a period of political transition. They'll come to an accord early next year. The governments will all sit down in Damascus and thrash out a load of economic plans that will benefit those in power. There'll be protests against it. Very violent protests. But it won't matter as everything's going to change next spring."

The eyes of Keith's co-workers fixed on him as he finished off his sandwich.

"What do you mean?" Susan asked.

"Hmmm?"

"What you just said. About Damascus and everything."

Keith shrugged. "Isn't that what they always do?"

There had been a brief pause as the point was considered before the topic of conversation had moved on to last night's *Coronation Street*.

As he rounded the corner onto his street, Keith pondered what he had said. He was no political commentator, not by a long shot. You got those chaps who had a view on everything and kept banging on about it continually, normally in the pub when they'd had a few. Keith shuddered. Alcohol was a terrible thing, indeed. It turned men into monsters, bringing out the brute that lay beneath the thin skin of social expectations. When people imbibed, they just let rip with all manner of pent-up prejudices and seething anxiety that they normally kept stoppered up in the bottle of polite repression. No, he wasn't one of those. What you saw with Keith Templeton was what you got: a middle-aged man in a simple nine-to-five job where he pushed figures around on a spreadsheet to make life easier for his co-workers. He didn't drink. He had no real opinions on anything outside of work or his family. He didn't even normally watch the news. Yes, he had the daily paper delivered, but that was more for the crossword. It paid to keep the old noodle active.

So why had he said what he had?

Was he changing in his old age? Was he subconsciously observing things around him, making notes and compiling opinions? He certainly hoped not! That seemed like a recipe for disaster. Opinions only caused arguments.

He was dragged out of his reverie by a scene of

commotion down the street. There were fire engines and police cars. His pace quickened as a queer sense of dread overcame him. Blue lights were strobing down the street as the leather soles of his shoes tapped against the asphalt. The iridescent colours flickered from house to house, casting each one in an unnerving hue.

All except one house.

His.

It was no longer there.

Where once had been his beautiful suburban detached homestead, was now a mess of burnt-out brick and timber. Collapsed beams jutted up from the centre of the debris like the scorched rib cage of some ancient behemoth. Smoke drifted up from its carcass, filling the early evening air with an acrid stench. An unspeakable monster had replaced his sanctuary from a crazed world of arguments and politics.

Keith's briefcase dropped to the floor as he staggered up to the blue and white tape surrounding the scene. He was aware of a firm arm gripping his elbow and turned to face a middle-aged, scruffy-looking man. The man was saying something, but Keith couldn't hear.

All that filled his ears was a pounding three-fold rhythm, a bizarre heartbeat that drowned out all around him. Deep inside his gut, something that had slept for a very long time was beginning to wake.

"My house..." he managed to force out of the mouth he wore. "My..." his racing mind that flooded with newly unlocked thoughts and memories struggled to find the correct word, "family?"

"Sir?" The shabbily dressed individual's words started to penetrate the fog of transformation that was smothering Templeton's form. A small black wallet was lifted up and flashed in front of him, showing official identification. Police. "Am I to understand this is your house?"

A pair of eyes glanced back at the ruin and a head nodded. "I…" It needed instruction. It needed protocol. "I need to sit down. Somewhere quiet."

The police officer nodded and led it to his car. It heard the sound of the human's keys jingling in the pocket of a pair of worn trousers. They rested next to a packet of something. Templeton's form flashed out its tongue and caught the scent of menthol-flavoured sweets. "My… family," the mouth repeated around the foreign, unnatural words.

"I am sorry, sir. We have found one set of remains. We think they belong to your wife, but there is something rather odd about them."

It nodded. Of course the remains would be odd. The effect of the inferno would have seen to that. "The… *boy…*" It almost spat the abhorrent word. "Where is he?"

The officer consulted his notes. "That's… Alec? That's what a neighbour told us?"

The shape of a middle-aged family man with an in-nocuous mundane job was aware that its heart had stopped beating, that the lungs were no longer inhaling, exhaling air. It forced its weak-looking head to nod as its simulacrum of eyes appeared to study the sack of flesh in front of it.

"No sign. At a guess, he'd not come home from school yet. We're working on the theory… that… the fire…" The officer's words dwindled to a confused halt as he watched the thing in front of him change form. The skin of the nondescript, blue-suited man rippled and shifted, its face transforming into that of the one that the DCI saw every morning when he vaguely scraped a razor over his

102

chin.

The police officer was aware of a sharp, quick movement then agonising pain before blackness overcame him.

The simulacrum of the DCI loosened the snake-like arm from around the crushed neck of the human and flexed its fingers as the limb returned into the form of a human arm. Using this newly-formed arm, it removed the contents of the officer's pockets before bundling the corpse into the boot of the car.

It turned towards the devastated home and nodded as new, pre-programmed instructions began to reveal themselves in what passed for its brain. The Twin had fled, aided by the Light. They would flee to the safe house in Scotland. It was to attempt to intervene there; apprehend the boy if possible and alter the course of events that had already happened. If it failed and the Twin escaped once again, it was to initiate its alternate mission.

The construct was to head to Lancaster.

To Spallucci.

Author's Notes

Well, here I am again, sitting down and tapping away at my keyboard, composing words that I wonder if anyone will actually read. That's the funny thing about an author's notes section. The author will have written their work in a flurry of creativity, get to the end, breathe and then suddenly think that there are certain things they need to explain or simply chat about. The reader, on the other hand, normally gets to the end of a story (or set of stories, as you just have), either nods in satisfaction or groans in frustration, closes the book, has a brew and starts on their next set of reading material (normally after going to the loo first).

I have to hold my hand up and say that I am just as guilty of this misdemeanour as everyone else. For example, I love Kathy Reichs' Temperance Brennan novels (the ones that inspired the amazing *Bones* television series). At the end of each novel, forensic anthropologist turned talented author has a few pages dedicated to explaining what influenced the stories. I think that, out of her numerous books, I have just read one set of author's notes. If Ms Reichs is reading this (which would be absolutely amazing, I hasten to add) I offer my complete and humble apology!

But, us author's do like to talk about our work, even if it is to the faceless void, so here are my little pieces of information about the stories that you've just read. If you do happen to carry on and read these little ramblings, why not make my heart beat faster with delight and let me know via social media? There are links on my website on the About The Author page.

Doing The Right Thing

The Archangel Michael is one of my oldest characters. As I've mentioned numerous times, I wrote a novel (I use that term in the loosest sense of the word) when I was a teenager. It was entitled *Fallen Angel*. Over the years it has evolved and grown alongside my ever-expanding universe and is now due for publication in about five years (at the time of writing). The main character was, and still is, Abaddon, an angel who was framed for the theft of the Eternals from Heaven before being cast into the sentient ocean that surrounds reality, the Abyss. Michael was Abaddon's best friend and failed him in his time of need, an act which has always haunted him.

When we catch up with Michael here we find him existing in the Divergent Lands after the Battle of Megiddo, an event that takes place in *Fallen Angel* but has been mentioned numerous times in the *Bobby Normal* books, such as the last time we bumped into the general of Heaven's army.

In *Bobby Normal and The Fallen*, Michael has a battered doll in his possession. This is the same doll from this short story and serves as a reminder that even if you do the right thing, people can suffer because of your actions — a theme that echoes throughout the Sam Spallucci stories.

Waste Not Want Not

This was a short story that I originally wrote for my previous anthology, *Out Of The Depths*. However, space limitations and the fact that I felt it wasn't finished meant that it got temporarily shelved. I came back to it in 2023, gave it a good polish and ended up with the story that you read here.

I enjoy writing in the first person as I feel we get to understand a character far more intimately and I had great fun developing cannibal Josh.

Hear My Scare is unusual in how many of the stories are either definitely or possibly in the Spalluciverse. *Waste Not Want Not* is one of the possible ones as it is set in the surrounding area and the murder of the shop worker takes place in Lancaster itself.

Servant of the Lord/Lessons Learned

As I'm sure you will have noticed, these two stories complement each other, effectively telling the story from two different points of view. The scene itself is one which takes place offstage, so to speak, in *The Case of the Crying Crucifix*, the final part of *Sam Spallucci: Lux Æterna*. There is a scene where Sam and Alec are rescued from the temple complex of Asmodeus by Katy Normal. Here we see how she infiltrated the stronghold of the male Fallen.

Katy is a character very close to my heart. If you haven't yet read the *Bobby Normal* books, please go away and do so now. Seriously. Right now! There are links on my website for the books. I love how her character develops over the first four books in the series. Here we see her about eight years later, having been under the tutelage and mentorship of Asherah. As I finish editing this book, I am knee-deep in writing *Sam Spallucci: Dare The Dragon* which deals with the aftermath of the *Bobby Normal* series and starts to look at what will become of Katy when the disturbed girl finally reaches adulthood in the *Divergent Lands* trilogy. I'll say no more for now as that way spoilers lie…

Craft

A few years ago, I had a chat with a reader about a dress that she'd made from old teabags. We had a chuckle about how it would be more sinister if the teabags, in turn, had been crafted from human flesh. That idea evolved into this piece of flash fiction.

Mother and Son

Oh, where to begin with this one?

Okay, so this story serves two main purposes for me. One is practical whereas the other is emotional.

On the practical side, I had to explain how Dave came into possession of Nightingale's photo of herself by the font. He shows it to Bobby and Katy in *Bobby Normal and the Children of Cain*. After publishing the book, I realised that I hadn't given him the damn thing yet! Hence we have the sweet scene on the roof where Night shows it to him before she heads off with Marcus to face Asmodeus, accidentally leaving it in her son's possession.

On the emotional side, I needed this as a way to bring to a conclusion the time that Night and Dave spend together. I won't say what happens in case you haven't read *Sam Spallucci: Lux Æterna*, but, well, let's just say I may have shed a tear after finishing the story.

Bubbles

This is one of the stories that feels like a complete standalone unless you notice the reference to the Damascus Accord, an event that has global consequences in the Spallucciverse. I love writing stories which can be a touch on the surreal or slightly insane side and this certainly fits that description with the idea of someone being able to steal bubbles.

Well, just take this story and tuck it away in your memory as it might get referred to in *Sam Spallucci: Dare The Dragon*. I'm just coming up to a scene where I introduce a new major side character and she could very well be the thief.

Lifting The Veil

This is a story that is planted firmly in the Spallucciverse garden. I've used Spud twice now in the main stories as well as seeing him in one short. I keep getting asked when he will get his own short story. Well, here it is.

As for the construct in the story and what he has been summoned to do? You'll have to wait for *Sam Spallucci: Dare The Dragon* to find out.

Appeasing The Gods

Another little dose of surrealism here, this time surrounding a painting. I've always had a phobia of paintings coming to life. I think this primarily comes from *Mezzotint* by M.R.James with the homicidal poacher and the brutal *Orange Is For Anguish, Blue For Insanity* by David Morrell. I play with this phobia here but really kitsch it up, so much so that the author of the piece destroys the little literary universe like a vengeful deity.

This is another one of the stories here that appear to be standalones, but are in fact part of the Spallucci-verse. The author, Luke Davies, is mentioned in *Sam Spallucci: Lux Æterna* as having been one of Sam's flat-mates at Luneside University. Watch out for his dramatic appearance in the final Sam book, *Sam Spallucci: Dance of Death*.

Metamorphosis
Right, the last one.

So, I ummed and ahhhed greatly before including this story in the anthology as it gives a humongous spoiler for *Sam Spallucci: Dare The Dragon*. Namely the identity of a certain Detective Chief Inspector. In the end, I decided to go with publishing it before *Dare,* and not after, to give the readers an insight into what will happen and let them cringe and hide behind cushions as the story unfolds, giving them more knowledge than poor old Sam Spallucci.

If you want more information about what has caused the fire then you need to read the novella *Child of Light* which came out in 2024 and tells the backstory of Sam's mysterious lodger, Alec.

Anyway, if you're still there, thank you for reading to the end. If you also happen to be Kathy Reichs, please let me know and I promise that I will go back and immediately read all your author notes whilst sitting under a cloud of shame.

So, don't forget to tell me what you think of this book. You can reach me through social media. And, please take a moment to hop over to Amazon and

Goodreads to leave a quick review or rating.

Take care and keep looking for what lurks in the shadows.

ASC January 2025.

About The Author

A.S.Chambers resides in Lancaster, England. He lives a fairly simple life of walking in the countryside, gazing at mountains and wondering if clouds taste of candy floss.

He is quite happy for, and in fact would encourage, you to follow him on Facebook, Instagram, Threads, TikTok, Patreon, Bluesky, Kickstarter and YouTube.

There is also a nice, shiny website:
www.aschambers.co.uk

www.ingramcontent.com/pod-product-compliance
Lightning Source LLC
Chambersburg PA
CBHW051709180726
48283CB00004B/1269